THE RE~~NO~~

Twin Bar Ran~~ch~~

Longtime Reno residents are stymied. Whatever possessed ~~reclusive rancher~~ Zane Dumas to turn his spread into a Hollywood movie set?

The Twin Bar, whose remote location is ideal for the Arabian horses Dumas raises, has taken on the look of a county fair. Semis and RVs line the long drive, and huge white tents have sprouted all over the property for the filming of *American Jack*, a classic Western scheduled for release next fall.

The film has been plagued with disaster from the start. Although box office megastar Ty Thomas plays the lead, rumors are rampant that the film's cowboy hero is afraid of horses. Two directors have already walked, and rookie Eve Caffrey has stepped in as the latest replacement.

~~Dumas say~~ yes? According to the movie crew members, the blond director's supermodel good looks may have had something to do with getting the rancher's approval. Though she's known as the Ice Princess to cast and crew, Eve Caffrey obviously knows how to turn on the heat to get what she wants.

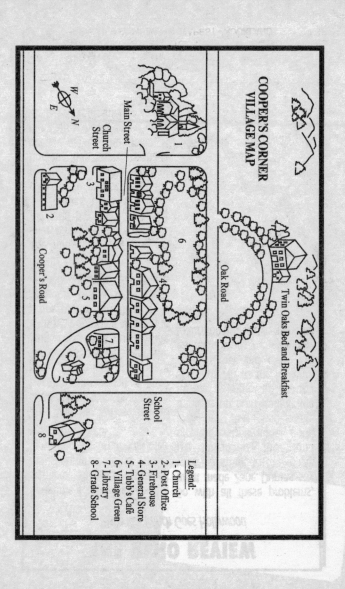

COOPER'S CORNER VILLAGE MAP

Twin Oaks Bed and Breakfast

Oak Road

Main Street

Church Street

Cooper's Road

School Street

Legend:
1- Church
2- Post Office
3- Firehouse
4- General Store
5- Tubb's Café
6- Village Green
7- Library
8- Grade School

COOPER'S CORNER

JANE PORTER

The Secret

HARLEQUIN®

TORONTO • NEW YORK • LONDON
AMSTERDAM • PARIS • SYDNEY • HAMBURG
STOCKHOLM • ATHENS • TOKYO • MILAN • MADRID
PRAGUE • WARSAW • BUDAPEST • AUCKLAND

For Zbyszek, Krysia and Kathy.
I love you.

HARLEQUIN BOOKS
225 Duncan Mill Road, Don Mills,
Ontario, Canada M3B 3K9

ISBN 0-373-61267-2

THE SECRET

Jane Porter is acknowledged as the author of this work.

Copyright © 2002 by Harlequin Books S.A.

Visit us at www.eHarlequin.com

Printed in U.S.A.

Dear Reader,

I jumped at the chance to participate in the COOPER'S CORNER series, especially when I discovered I'd be writing about a brooding American cowboy named Zane Dumas. I grew up spending vacations on my grandfather's cattle ranch in central California, and there's nothing sexier in my mind than a rough-and-tumble hero in boots, faded T-shirt and tight jeans.

But America isn't just about cowboys and rugged ranches. America also represents the dream of a new life—a better life—and my heroine, Eve Caffrey, is willing to fight for her dream.

Zane and Eve's story is for all those who believe in second chances, opportunity and hard work. It's also dedicated to my brother-in-law, Zbyszek Sikora, who emigrated from Poland in search of a better life and a bigger dream.

Yours,

Jane Porter

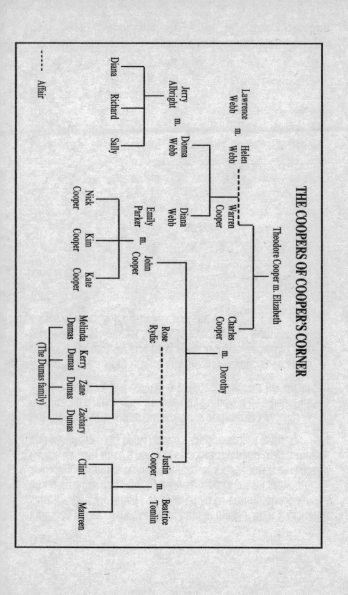

THE COOPERS OF COOPER'S CORNER

Theodore Cooper m. Elizabeth

Lawrence Webb m. Helen Webb

Warren Cooper ----- Donna Webb m. Jerry Albright

Diana — Richard — Sally

Charles Cooper m. Dorothy

Diana Webb

John Cooper m. Emily Parker

Nick Cooper — Kim Cooper — Kate Cooper

Rose Rydic ----- Justin Cooper m. Beatrice Tomlin

Melinda Dumas — Kerry Dumas — Zane Dumas — Zachary Dumas

(The Dumas family)

Clint — Maureen

----- Affair

CHAPTER ONE

"EXCUSE ME, SIR. Do you know where I can find Zane Dumas?"

Zane stiffened, tipped his Stetson back on his head and glanced toward the voice coming from outside the corral. A distinctively feminine face peered through the wooden railings. Wisp of wheat-blond hair. High cheekbones. Soft mouth. Female, all right.

He slung the lead rope over his shoulder and gave the young stallion a we're-not-finished-here look. The soft dirt poofed beneath Zane's boots as he headed for the split rail fence.

"Can I help you, ma'am?" he asked grimly. It was hotter than blazes and he swiped his wet forehead, thinking he didn't smell pretty.

"This is the Twin Bar Ranch, isn't it?"

A bead of sweat trickled down his back, and his white cotton T-shirt clung to his skin. He'd been in the corral all morning, first with a nervous filly, and now with a spirited stallion. He loved his Arabians but they were notoriously sensitive, and right now he was tired to the bone. "It is."

"I'm trying to track down the owner, a Mr. Dumas. Do you know where I can find him?"

"Right here." Zane whacked a hand against his back pocket, knocking off the dust, before extending it through the fence. "Zane Dumas. Something I can do for you?"

She stared at his hand for a split second, her pale forehead furrowing before she shook it. "Eve Caffrey," she said, her voice all business now.

Her hand felt small in his, but that was no surprise. He was built big, tall and solid, even for a cowboy. "I know that name."

Her smile looked tight. "You should. I left you a couple messages last week. I'm with Studioworks in Hollywood, California."

So that's what this was about. The movie they wanted to shoot on his ranch. The movie they were supposed to shoot nearly three months ago while he was gone.

Frustration welled and he clamped his jaw shut. He didn't have time for this. Didn't need the hassle, either. Releasing her hand, he hooked his thumbs around his belt loops. "You're wasting your time."

"You have a contract with Studioworks, Mr. Dumas."

"*Had* a contract, Miss Caffrey, and I've been through this with your folks already. Don't you people talk?"

Her blue eyes narrowed, and she didn't look quite so young anymore. There was an edge in the blue-green depths, a resolve that only came with time, and experience. "I believe you were notified that we needed to extend the shoot dates."

"I didn't sign the new contract."

"Your ranch foreman did."

"And he's been replaced." Ramón's leaving had nothing to do with the film studio, but Zane didn't bother to mention that.

Eve appeared momentarily at a loss for words, but then she asked, "Is there some other place we could talk?"

He knew what she wanted, but he wasn't in the mood for a hard sale or a soft proposition. He'd left for South America in the spring to check out different breeders and had returned a month ago to a series of small disasters on his horse ranch. Losing Ramón was one of them, and even though Zane wished his long-time ranch manager happiness, things were a hell of a lot harder without his help.

Zane didn't want to be ugly, but he had enough on his plate at the moment, and the last thing he needed was a bunch of Hollywood types tramping all over the place. "I know what you want, ma'am, and the answer is still no."

"Give me fifteen minutes."

"I've already given you five, and I don't feel any different than I did before. Another ten won't change my mind, either."

"Please."

Now she was going to start on the sweet talk. He hated this more than the hard sell. "It's not going to work," he said, tugging the brim of his hat lower.

"What's not going to work?" she asked, hands on her hips, her silvery-blond head tipped sideways.

His gaze slid over her tall, slim figure. She was dressed conservatively, dark trousers, blazer, knit blouse, but the tailored clothes did little to hide the curves of her hips and thighs and high, full breasts. "This," he said curtly, nodding at her. "The woman-thing."

"Woman-thing," she repeated.

"I don't fall for it. Doesn't work with me—"

"What doesn't work?" Her voice had risen a notch.

"Sugar and spice," he answered, and was immediately rewarded with an icy glare.

"You're talking nursery rhymes, Mr. Dumas, and I'm trying to talk business."

He'd hit a sore spot with her. Fine. She'd hit a sore spot with him, too. He'd already told the director no, and he didn't need some leggy blonde with flashing blue-green eyes and sexier-than-sin lips driving out and trying to sweet-talk him into changing his mind. "What part of no don't you understand?"

She exhaled slowly. "The part where the film gets shelved because you've changed your mind—"

"I didn't change my mind. You and your people didn't show."

"Mr. Dumas," she said, softening her tone, "I've just been hired to replace the last director and my back is against the wall. I've been up three nights straight rewriting a script that had far too many treatments, while my production crew sits around the hotel doing nothing but eating nachos and playing Nintendo."

"That's not my problem, Miss…"

"Caffrey." She drew herself tall, squared her shoulders. "Look, I'm not looking for a freebie or a handout. We're paying for the use of your ranch. Studioworks agreed—"

"To shoot here four months ago. You were scheduled to be here in May. It's September now."

"There were production delays."

"I'm sorry about that. I really am, but this is a busy time for me here. I'm short-staffed and I'm not about to turn my life upside down for your little movie."

Anger blazed in her eyes. "My little movie?"

Zane sucked in a swift breath, surprised and intrigued by the burst of blue fire in her eyes. He hadn't seen that kind of emotion in a long time.

A very long time.

He stared at her for a moment, considering her request, and ultimately rejected the notion. He couldn't have a bunch of people swarming all over his ranch, not here, not now, not the way he was feeling.

Which was like hell. He'd hoped his months away would have calmed him, focused him, but instead he just felt angrier. More disoriented. How much time did a person need to get over the grieving and back to living? It'd been five years.

But did five years of grief absolve him of a crime? It was a crime, too. He just hadn't been arrested. And while no one had come out and called him a murderer to his face, he knew what people thought.

Worse yet, he knew the truth.

No, he definitely couldn't handle a bunch of California-types here now. "I'm sorry."

She gave him a look that stirred something in his gut. For a moment he felt like an ass. Someone hard and cruel and unjust. "So that's that?"

"Afraid so."

She handed him a card. "I'm staying downtown at the Nevada Suites if you change your mind."

"I won't change my mind."

Her gaze met his and held. Zane saw fatigue in her eyes, and something else. Worry? Fear? Then she smiled, her lips curving crookedly, and the clouds vanished. "Thank you, Mr. Dumas."

He inclined his head and she turned away to walk back to her car. His narrowed gaze followed the subtle swing of her hips.

Glancing down at the card she handed him, he read

her name. Eve Caffrey. Eve as in Adam and Eve. Eve as in all woman.

He watched as she swung open the car door and slid behind the wheel. His stomach knotted, and the muscles tensed throughout his body. Oh, yes, she was definitely all woman. Every dangerous, voluptuous inch of her.

HOT, HOT, HOT. It had to be at least eighty-something, and of course her rental car's air conditioner chose this moment to go on the blink. *Damn.*

Knowing it was futile, Eve twisted the dashboard dials again, begging the air conditioning to kick in. *A little bit, just give me a little bit.* But the fan only blew hot, dry air.

Swearing beneath her breath, she reluctantly rolled down both windows to let the warm air circulate. Her shoulder-length hair blew around her head, in her eyes, and reaching up, she tugged a tendril back, firmly tucking it behind one ear. *What a waste of a day.*

Make that two days wasted now. Two days and the clock was ticking. Every minute was precious. Ty Thomas was scheduled to shoot another film December first, and his agent had made it clear that he would be on the other movie set whether or not *American Jack* had finished production. That meant she had two months to get this movie made.

Blinking grit from her eyes, she gripped the steering wheel tighter, wanting desperately to believe that she could pull this off even though the last two directors had failed.

She wouldn't admit it to anyone, but she was scared. She'd waited her whole life for a chance to direct a ''big'' movie, and this film was it: big story, big star, big budget.

Big mess.

It took her exactly one day on the job to realize she'd agreed to direct a disaster—and for next to no money. That was the funny part. She was so excited to be directing this film that she'd waived the salary, declining to be paid a flat fee up front and choosing to take a percentage of the film's box-office gross instead.

Only the way things were going, there wouldn't be any gross. There wouldn't even be a film.

She felt as if she'd just climbed on board the *Titanic* minutes before it went under. If this film sank—she'd sink with it. Hollywood was superstitious and doubly hard on women. No one would remember that she'd stepped in at the last minute to tackle *American Jack* after two directors walked in less than six months. No, they'd just remember it was her name on the production and her fiasco.

But she wouldn't direct a disaster, and she wasn't going to go under, either. She'd worked too damn hard to fail now.

ZANE SLUNG A BIG BALL of barbed wire out of the back of the truck. Thick leather work gloves protected his hands as he carried the wire to the fence. This was work he could do in his sleep. He'd grown up on this property, knew the land inside and out.

The sun beat down on his head as he unraveled the ball of wire. His insides felt almost as tangled. That woman—Eve what's-her-name—had tied him into knots. He hated the tension inside of him. Hated extra frustration. This was exactly what he didn't need.

Another truck bounced up the rough dirt road, kicking up clouds of dust, then came to a stop. Zach swung out of the cab, walking toward Zane with the slightly bowlegged gait of a man who spent his life in the saddle.

"Need a hand?" Zach asked, tugging on his own leather gloves.

"I'm all right."

Zach's eyebrows rose as the flexed wire fencing slipped from Zane's grasp, snapping back on his wrists. Zane uttered some choice words.

"Hurts like hell, doesn't it?" Zach said, grabbing the wire and stretching it out again.

Zane looked up at his twin brother from beneath the brim of his hat. Suddenly he knew they weren't talking about getting poked by barbed wire. This was about Jen. "Don't want to talk about it."

Zach's green eyes narrowed. "You can't bring her back. She's gone. She's been gone a long time."

A familiar pain wrapped Zane's heart in a viselike grip. Nothing in his life had prepared him for losing Jenny, but talking about her didn't help. It just made the fire inside him worse. "Hold the post steady," he said, taking a hammer and nail to the twisted wire.

Zach braced the post. "You can't run away forever."

Zane lifted the hammer and sank the nail with one swift blow. "I'm not running away from anything. I'm here, I'm working, and I'm taking care of business. You got a problem with that?"

"Yeah, actually, I do have a problem with you not returning phone calls. I have a problem that you won't make time for dinner with the family."

"I've just been busy."

"Too busy for us."

"Don't make this personal," Zane warned.

"But it *is* personal. We're your family and you don't even want to be part of our lives anymore. It's as if you can't stand the fact that we might have found some happiness—"

"Bullshit."

"Melinda's engaged, Kerry's madly in love," he continued, as though Zane hadn't spoken. "I've got someone I want to marry, someone you'd really like if you just gave her a chance, but instead of spending time with us, you've shut everyone out."

Zane drove another nail home. Sweat beaded his brow, and his shirt stuck to his back. "That's not it at all."

"No? Sure feels like it."

At last he straightened and pushed back the brim of his hat. He felt so damn tired he couldn't even speak. He didn't know what Zach wanted, didn't know what anyone wanted from him anymore.

Zach studied his brother for a long, tense moment, then slowly shook his head. "Jen would hate what you've become."

Zane's gaze locked with his brother's, but still he didn't say anything. He couldn't.

With a sigh, Zach drew his truck key from his pocket. "Leslie and I are going to meet Kerry and John for dinner."

"That's nice."

"Everyone wants to see you."

"I've got a lot to do—" Zane broke off, seeing the mute anger and frustration in his brother's eyes. Zach had expected his refusal, and he wasn't just angry, he was disappointed.

The two brothers had been so close. As kids, they'd done everything together. Zane swallowed hard, seeing now that it wasn't just Zach he'd alienated, but the rest of the family, his friends, even his ranch hands—which was one of the chief reasons Ramón had wanted to move on. Yeah, he was getting married, but the gentle foreman had had it with Zane's dark moods and endless expeditions to foreign countries.

Zane let out a slow, tense breath. "What time are you meeting?"

"Seven. Carmen's downtown."

Their family's favorite Mexican restaurant. The place he and his brother had always wanted to go for their birthday dinner when they were boys. "I'll see what I can do."

"You can do better than that."

"Fine. Seven. I'll be there."

Three hours later, showered and dressed in clean jeans and a faded denim shirt, Zane drove into downtown Reno. The sun was just setting as he locked up his truck.

Pocketing his keys, he stepped into the old adobe restaurant built nearly forty years ago in the popular style of a Southwest hacienda. The beige stucco walls were beginning to show their age, and in places the plaster was cracked, forming fine, spiderlike veins, but to Zane, Carmen's was home.

He hadn't wanted to come tonight, but now that he was here, with the gentle whir of the ceiling fans blowing cool air and the familiar spicy smell of roasted peppers, he felt good. Better than he had all day. Maybe he did need to get out more. Maybe he had cut himself off from his family too much.

EVE SAW THE LONG SHADOW stretch across the terracotta floor, even before she heard the tap of boots.

Shoulders that broad belonged to only one man.

Closing her menu, she pushed it aside and watched the restaurant hostess lead Zane Dumas through the courtyard toward a corner table.

She wasn't the only one who'd noticed his arrival. The group at her table stopped talking for a split second to watch the tall cowboy walk by. "Wow," the makeup artist whistled beneath her breath. "There's a real man for you."

Soft laughter followed, yet Eve couldn't crack a smile. He might be gorgeous, but he was also a huge thorn in her side at the moment. She'd given up sleeping to pound out a clean, tight script with a new writer she'd brought on board, but what good was a great script if they couldn't start filming?

Eve could still hear Zane's words ringing in her head. *It's not going to work.... The woman-thing,* and *I'm not about to turn my life upside down for your little movie.*

Her temper soared. She'd met a lot of opinionated men in Hollywood and worked with her share of egoists, too, but this guy really took the cake.

In all fairness, though, she couldn't criticize Zane Dumas's desire to protect his privacy. She was extremely private, too, and very focused on her work.

Maybe too focused, a tiny voice inside her whispered, and she grimaced. She wasn't a workaholic, and just because Nathan had called her one in the fight that led to their breakup didn't make him right. Yes, she did work hard. No, she wasn't married to her job. And just because she didn't feel compelled to settle down didn't mean she was cold or calculating.

There were still double standards, she thought with a small sigh. Men who worked extremely hard and made sacrifices for their career were considered tough, successful, talented and capable. Women who worked hard and made similar choices were judged as driven, power-hungry, controlling. Why could a man pursue his dream, but a woman was supposed to settle for less?

She was gritting her teeth again, when she heard one of her lighting guys dare a woman at their table to approach the cowboy and make a pass at him.

"He's expecting others," the wardrobe assistant answered with a grin. "Although hell, I'd love to sit on *his* lap."

Everyone at their table laughed and turned to look at Zane, their eyes traveling the length of him as if taking inventory.

Zane had pulled out his chair and was starting to sit down when he must have felt them staring at him. Glancing up, he looked their way. His narrowed gaze skimmed the long table cluttered with glasses and plates before settling on Eve.

He stared at her so hard and long she couldn't breathe. The air bottled in her lungs. His green gaze went straight through her, as though he were searching for something. A shiver raced down her spine and the hair at her nape rose. This wasn't a man to be ignored.

His lips twisted a fraction of an inch, before he nodded briefly in her direction and sat down, dropping his hat on the table beside him.

Contact broken, Eve sagged into her chair. She didn't know what she expected, or hoped would happen, and the intensity of her emotions stunned her.

For a moment there, she'd almost liked the attention. For a moment, she'd wanted him to look.

Why?

She gave her head a brief, frustrated shake. The movie, of course. She'd hoped he'd changed his mind. Hoped he'd reconsidered.

But that didn't explain the faint tremor in her hand as she reached for her margarita and lifted it to her lips. She drank the icy citrus-and-tequila cocktail in great swallows, trying for a calm she didn't feel. She really needed a good night's sleep, but she wasn't going to get it until her crew was working again.

"I'll go talk to him," Eve said, turning to look at her crew, aware that she was still considered an outsider. They'd been working on this production for nearly two and a half months, and they'd been through the wringer with the last two directors. They didn't expect anything good from her, either.

"You'll go?" one of the gaffers mocked. "Ice Princess?"

The others laughed, and a couple of the guys slapped each other on the shoulder as if highly entertained.

Eve wasn't sure what she felt, only that she couldn't afford to be weak in front of them. "I'm not an ice princess," she said, licking the salt that was on her finger from the rim of her glass. "I'm an ice *queen*. And if you think I'm afraid to approach the cowboy, well, you just watch."

She pushed up from the table, knuckles briefly braced against the wooden surface. Approaching Zane Dumas again, in public, was asking for humiliation, but she didn't have a choice. There was no way she could drag her crew up to Gerlach, some one hundred and sixty miles north, to shoot. The area had the old buildings and terrain she needed, but not the facilities. Dumas' property was perfect for the film, and it was only a half hour drive outside of Reno.

As she crossed the restaurant floor, her leather heels clicking against the glazed tiles, it flashed through her mind that one day she'd get smart and not take so many risks. But until then, she'd keep living on the edge.

As Eve neared Zane's table, he was studying the menu, his dark brown brows pulled down in concentration. Her heart did a strange double thump, nerves uncomfortably taut.

He wasn't going to appreciate her persistence. He wasn't going to respect her ambition. But she couldn't quit. She didn't know how.

CHAPTER TWO

"GOOD EVENING, MR. DUMAS."

He shot her a quizzical look before slowly rising. "Miss Caffrey."

She hadn't realized how tall he was until she craned her head back to better see his face. He wasn't just tall, he was built big, solid, thickly muscled. *Like a mountain,* she thought, rather amazed that he could make her feel small when she was five ten. Most men in Hollywood weren't tall, even the leading male actors. Her Australian star, Ty Thomas, was one of the few men who actually had some height, and he was the exception.

"You've discovered Carmen's, I see," Zane said, his deep voice husky enough to send a strange vibration through her.

"We eat here every night. It's become the crew's favorite hangout."

"There're no video games here."

He'd remembered her flippant remark from earlier. "But there are nachos."

"Great nachos," he corrected her before smiling faintly.

She found herself staring at his mouth. He had a beautiful mouth. The camera lens would love his face. "Can I buy you a drink?"

Zane hooked his thumbs over his belt buckle. "I don't drink."

"I should hire you. You'd be a good influence on the set." But Eve knew that her star, Ty, needed more than a good influence. He required a full-time handler. His drinking was out of control. He didn't know his lines. He showed up drunk and belligerent, and the last director ended up in a fistfight with him—but it was the director who got fired, not Ty, which showed Eve quite clearly who wielded the power on this production.

"I haven't changed my mind, Miss Caffrey."

She managed a smile. "Didn't think you had, but I don't give up easily."

"I see." Turning away, Zane scanned the restaurant. "Your friends are watching," he added, nodding toward her table.

Eve glanced over her shoulder to see the dozen pair of eyes riveted their way. The crew looked like kids, mouths agape. They didn't know Eve well, but they hadn't expected her to put herself out there in the line of fire. "They're taking bets," she said lightly.

"Bets?" Zane repeated.

"It's a way they kill time. They bet on everything. Little things. Nothing. Anything to make conversation and get a laugh." When he didn't say anything, she swallowed. "It's kind of crazy, I know—"

"I get it," he answered, pulling out a chair and propping a boot on the bottom rung. "So what would they be betting on now?"

She felt heat creep into her cheeks. "They're wondering if you'll leave with me."

"Leave with you?"

"Sleep with me."

His dark brows lifted. "We just met."

"Doesn't matter in L.A. If you're beautiful—" she could feel her face burning "—or unusual, anything can happen."

His expression cleared, understanding dawning. "They don't know who I am."

"No. They've no clue. Only my assistant director would recognize you, and he's not here tonight. He's back at the hotel calling real estate agents, trying to find another place we could shoot. But he won't find another place that's as good as your ranch. I want your ranch and I'm willing to negotiate the contract Studioworks wrote up. Just tell me what you need."

A tiny muscle popped at his jaw. "I need you all to clear out of town and leave me alone."

Eve glanced at the table where the film crew was still sitting. They were grinning at her like fools. She caught sight of the pile of dollar bills growing on the table and swore beneath her breath. They *were* taking bets.

Zane had noticed the mound of money, too. "So they do think you're trying to pick me up."

She flushed. "It's entertainment."

"And you're Hollywood."

He really wasn't going to make this easy for her. "Why do you dislike me so much?"

"I don't dislike you." His expression looked hard, but his voice was pitched low and sounded husky. "I respect you. It can't be easy being a young female director in your business. Hell, it's not easy in any business, but I don't see Hollywood being especially kind to women."

Those words, and the way he said them, hit her square in the chest, creating the most intense rush of emotion. For a man who didn't like to talk much, he'd just proved himself surprisingly sensitive. "It's not." She tried to smile. "And I'm in trouble."

She hadn't meant to say that. She was rarely so brutally honest with anyone, but the words slipped out. And now that she'd been honest, what did she have to lose by telling him the truth? "I'm not a director with clout," she added quietly, trying hard to suppress all emotion. "I'm a replacement director on a film that's gone bad. But funny enough, this is also my big break. Maybe my only break. I've got to make the most of the opportunity—and I will."

He didn't say anything. He just looked at her.

"Give me five minutes, Mr. Dumas. Let me at least try to address your concerns. Maybe I can answer some questions you have. I just want five minutes."

Slowly he studied her face, and the color burning across her cheekbones in hot waves. She felt the weight of his inspection, felt the close, critical scrutiny as his eyes settled on hers, then on her nose, her mouth. "You've got five minutes," he said at length. "Have a seat."

Eve's heart raced. She saw a bit of blue sky. Maybe, just maybe, things would work out after all. She sat down and Zane faced her across the round table set for five. "You've got guests coming."

He nodded. "Family. But my brother's usually late and I'm usually early. We have plenty of time."

The waiter arrived and Zane ordered an iced tea. Eve ordered one, as well. "I don't mind if you drink," Zane said. "You could have ordered something else."

"I'm fine," she said, sitting forward. She couldn't help thinking about Ty and his alcohol problem. If only he'd cut back, or cut it out altogether. "Did you ever drink?" she asked Zane.

He hesitated a moment. "I've never been a big drinker, but something happened a few years back and I haven't touched the stuff since."

There was a story behind his answer. Zane was full of stories, she thought. Stories and mysteries. She didn't want to like him, but there was something larger than life about him, something intriguing. Maybe it was the contradictions in him. Behind the muscle and strength she glimpsed gentleness.

He might walk and talk tough, but he wasn't cruel.

And he was giving her a chance to pitch the movie, and what she needed. But before she could speak, the waiter returned with chips, salsa and their iced tea. Once he left, she jumped right in. "Your property is perfect for our film. The outbuildings, the corrals, the terrain—it's exactly what we need."

"You could find almost the same thing up in Gerlach," he said. "And they'd love to have you up there."

So he knew the folks in Gerlach had contacted her. "But there aren't any accommodations for my cast or crew. We'd be pitching tents, and without running water and electricity, we'd never make it. We're too big a group, and the crew has had too many days off. They're at one another's throats. They need to work. They need to get back on the job."

He studied his ice tea. "What do you know about a working ranch? Or horses?"

"Not much."

"So what makes you think you can make a western?"

Eve slid her fingers down the cool, damp stem of

the goblet. "I believe anyone can do anything if they try hard enough."

"Ranching's a hard life. Working the land, working with animals—it's unpredictable. Some years crops don't grow. Other years mares miscarry and there's no rhyme nor reason. There are no guarantees. Everything's a crapshoot."

"You could be talking about my life. But then, I was brought up in this business. My dad's a director. I knew what I was getting into." Her lips twisted. "Or I should say, I thought I knew what I was getting into."

"And I was brought up on a ranch."

"Yeah?"

He nodded. "The Twin Bar. My parents once owned the spread but divided it among us kids when they retired."

"You have brothers and sisters?"

"Two sisters and a twin brother."

"Twin?" Hard to believe there was another man like this. She pictured the way Zane had looked at the corral earlier, all hard planes and glistening muscles. She'd been fascinated by the dampness of his T-shirt, the dust on his boots, the snug fit of his faded jeans. He hadn't been what she expected. He still wasn't.

"Identical twins," he added, his voice a deep, soft drawl.

"What's he like?"

Zane laughed, and the husky timbre brought a second flood of warmth to her cheeks. She felt acutely aware of him, of his size, of his strength, of the differences between them.

"Nice," Zane said, still laughing. "Zach's a nice guy. Folks usually like him."

I bet, she thought. *If he looks half as good as you do.*

His dusty-green eyes met hers. "Tell me more about the movie."

As his gaze held hers, heat washed through her limbs, heat and something else. She was responding to him at such an elemental level. She'd always been comfortable with men; she'd had her share of relationships, but she'd never felt this kind of attraction before. She, Eve Caffrey, was all business, all the time, and yet right now she was feeling anything but businesslike. "What specifically do you want to know?" she asked, her own voice huskier than usual.

Zane's eyes narrowed. "Why my place?"

"I need an authentic horse ranch. I don't want pretty picket fences, or lots of whitewashed buildings. I want rugged. I need rugged. This is a period piece. It's Old West, turn of the century, end of the American frontier. Not just any place will do. We scouted the west for months and we zeroed in on the Twin Bar because the stone buildings on your property are the real thing, part of an old fort that once housed calvary officers."

"How much time are you talking?"

Was that a yes? Eve's pulse quickened. She sat up a little straighter. "Four weeks, maybe six."

"Six weeks is a long time to have strangers underfoot."

"I'd make sure the crew stayed out of your way. They'd know it's a working horse ranch, and that your business comes first."

He fell silent again, then finally gave his head a slow shake. "I have mares about to foal, one of them very high-strung and sensitive to change."

"We can stay clear of your barn, and I'll do my best to shoot around your schedule—"

"You don't even know my schedule."

"Then tell me. Show me. Let me understand what you want and I'll make sure we work with you."

"You say that now—"

"I mean it, too. I never make a promise I don't intend to keep."

His gaze met hers and held. She felt the tension in him, felt his ambivalence, as well. He didn't want to do this and yet he didn't want to make things harder for her, either. On the one hand, he was a rough-and-tumble cowboy, and on the other, a gentleman.

"When would you want to start?"

She felt a bubble of pure elation as her bit of blue sky broke wide open. "Tomorrow."

His brow furrowed. "Then let's agree on some ground rules. My house—obviously off-limits. My ranch hands need a place to go that's private, so you can film the exterior of the bunkhouse, but nothing inside. You can bring in the necessary trucks, tents and equipment, but you need to remember this is a working horse ranch and the ranch is to be left in the same condition you found it—or better."

She nodded. "Agreed."

"When you're done shooting each day, I want everybody to clear out. No loitering. No drinking or drugs on my property. No fighting, either."

"Got it." She waited to see if he'd add anything else, but when he didn't, Eve stood up and stretched out her hand. "It's a deal. And thank you, Mr. Dumas. I'm very grateful."

ZACH AND LESLIE APPEARED as Eve returned to her table. Zach stared after Eve, surprised, almost puzzled.

Zane caught his brother's expression. "What's wrong?" he asked, rising from the table to greet Leslie with a kiss.

Zach frowned and shook his head. "I don't know. She looks familiar. Does she live around here?"

"No. Hollywood. Name's Eve Caffrey. She's a film director."

Zach's brows furrowed deeper, but anything he wanted to say was cut short by the arrival of Kerry, who'd come alone.

"John was called into a last-minute meeting," she explained with a shrug. "The life of a deputy sheriff. But not to worry, he'll join us later if he can. And Melinda called me again to apologize for not coming, but both the kids are sick."

With everyone seated again, Zach ordered a pitcher of margaritas and Zane asked for a refill on his iced tea. As everyone munched on the chips and salsa, Zane glanced around the table and realized that Zach was right. His family was happy, happier than he'd seen them in a long time. Good. They deserved it. There'd been some hard years, and a little more heartbreak than one family needed. But now his dad was feeling better, and his brother and sisters had found love. You couldn't ask for more than that.

As if able to read his mind, Zach leaned forward, raising his tall green goblet, the thick rim sparkling with salt. "To the future."

"To a *great* future," Leslie added, and the others echoed the toast, clinking glasses.

Zane joined in with his iced tea glass, yet he glanced swiftly away, looking toward the long table across the restaurant where Eve had been sitting with her crew. The table was empty. They'd gone.

He felt the most peculiar sense of loss, and he drew a slow breath, wondering what the hell was wrong with him. All day his emotions had run hot and cold. Even now everything inside him felt stirred up.

Zach and Leslie looked at each other, exchanging silent, knowing glances. Zane didn't miss the wordless exchange. Zach had something on his mind.

"What's up?" Zane asked, wondering for the first time if this dinner get-together wasn't more than just a casual thing.

"I've been trying to figure out a way to tell you this," Zach said, sitting forward, arms braced on the edge of the table, "but there's never been a good moment, and every time I try to start to tell you, something comes up."

"You're going to marry the beautiful and talented Dr. Leslie Hall?" Zane guessed, breaking into a grin.

Leslie and Zach exchanged another look, this one full of love. "Not yet," Leslie answered softly, cheeks rosy.

"But soon. We hope. *I hope.*" Zach leaned over and kissed Leslie. "But this isn't about Leslie and me. It's about us, and Mom and Dad."

Zane didn't speak, and he noticed that Kerry wasn't eating chips anymore. In fact, no one was eating or drinking, and all eyes were fixed on him. "Dad having heart problems again?" he asked quietly, feeling a hint of fear.

"No," Zach answered quickly. "This actually goes back a long, long way. Leslie was the one who first discovered this."

Zane waited for the rest.

Pausing a moment, Zach drew a breath, then blurted the words. "Mom and Dad aren't our biological parents."

What? Zane shook his head, certain he hadn't heard right. "Say that again."

Zach pulled an old black-and-white photograph from his shirt pocket. "This is our biological mother. Her name is Rose Rydic, and this man, we think, is our father."

"Mom and Dad are our parents. Mom had us at the West View Rural Clinic in Reno. Dr. Keller delivered us."

"You were switched at birth," Leslie interjected gently. "Dr. Keller was my dad, and when your mom gave birth, her baby was stillborn. This woman in the photo, Rose Rydic, died just after delivering you and Zach. My dad couldn't bear to tell Eleanor that she'd lost another baby, and since Rose had no husband, no family, he placed you two in Eleanor's arms, and since that moment you've been hers."

"Damn straight." Zane felt a flood of heat through his limbs, his temper barely leashed. "I don't need or want other parents. I'm a Dumas. That's good enough for me."

Zach's brow creased. "I know this is a shock—it was for all of us, Mom and Dad, too. But aren't you curious about where we came from, who are real parents—"

"Dad and Mom are our real parents—"

"I meant, biological parents. We have another history, another family—"

"I don't," Zane interrupted flatly. "I'm not interested."

"It's all right," Kerry said, reaching out and laying

a hand on his forearm. Though the Dumas siblings considered Kerry their sister, she was in fact their cousin. Eleanor and Hamilton had adopted Kerry after her parents were killed when she was only five. She'd always been the sensitive one, and she obviously shared an understanding of what Zane was going through at the moment.

"You don't have to do anything," she added calmly. "Zach just thought you would want to know."

Why would he want to know? Zane asked himself several hours later, after returning home. He shut the front door, locking it behind him and switching on the hall light.

It had never crossed his mind that he wasn't a Dumas, Eleanor and Hamilton's son. He *liked* his parents. He *respected* his parents. They were the kind of people he wanted to be, the kind of people who'd give the shirt off their back to help a fellow human being.

Zach had sent the photograph home with him, and Zane pulled it out of his denim shirt pocket and held it up to the hall light.

He stared at the faces in the photo, trying to be as objective as possible. The couple looked young—the woman was hardly more than a girl, late teens, early twenties. Zane saw beauty in the curve of her mouth and in the shape of her eyes, but he felt nothing.

The man in the photograph was tall, broad-shouldered, fit. He had strong features, but again Zane felt nothing. They were strangers to him.

They'd remain strangers, too.

Dropping the photograph on the living room mantel, Zane turned off the house lights and went to bed.

EVE SAT IN BED, the hotel table lamp on, rereading the script. The week of grueling work had paid off. The dialogue was smooth, much more natural, closer to the way it read in the book. The scenes were logical, too. A book rarely translated neatly to the screen, but in this case, the script Eve had inherited didn't even resemble the original story.

The novel had been a runaway success, hitting number one on the bestseller list and remaining there over fifteen weeks. *American Jack* was a period piece set in the West, but more important, it was a story about the land, and fate, dreams and disappointment, and finding one's place in the world.

Maybe she wasn't a cowgirl, but she understood a story like this. It was her story, and her father's story. It was a story they both were born to tell.

Eve's heart ached for a moment. Her dad would have killed for a chance to do a movie like this. He had spent his whole life perfecting his craft, hoping against hope that he'd be given a real story, and a real budget. The chance had never come.

Impulsively, she reached for the phone and dialed home. Her father answered. Her mother was already in bed. "Eva," he said, using the Polish derivative of Eve.

"Did I wake you?" she asked.

"No. I'm up," her father answered. "Finishing a movie."

"What movie?"

"*Potop,* of course."

"Of course." She smiled a little. Despite the forty years he'd spent in the States, his Polish accent was still thick. He'd emigrated as a twenty-year-old, leaving Poland via Vienna while participating in a government-sponsored trip for young filmmakers.

Even though her father had been considered a promising young talent, and was well respected in Poland, he hadn't wanted to work with the hard-line government. He'd wanted more opportunity, more creative freedom, better economic conditions.

Eventually he'd found work in Hollywood, but it had never been the kind of work he craved. He had a unique vision of the world, yet the language barrier and his reclusive nature hadn't translated well to the Southern California scene. Hollywood was built on money, reputation and connections. Eve's father had none of the three.

"You're going to do fine," her dad said brusquely, instinctively picking up on her anxiety. Yet he would never baby her. He was a tough man, a strong man, and he'd pushed his daughters to be the same. "Worrying won't help you. Only work will. You have to get your crew back to work."

"I am. We start again tomorrow."

"Good. Now, do justice to the story. Honor the words, the truth, the emotions. That's real filmmaking."

"You make it sound easy."

"If filmmaking were easy, everybody would do it."

She smiled reluctantly, picturing her father's expression. His thick white hair would be standing on end, his bushy salt-and-pepper eyebrows drawn together over blue eyes that spit fire and ice. His heart was like that, too, intense emotions, more storm than calm. He felt everything deeply, passionately, and she loved that about him.

Her father would have done justice to this film. He might have been born in Kazimierz Dolny, a small medieval town eighty miles outside of Warsaw, but he was American to the bone. He loved his adopted country, believed so much in the opportunity here. Believed vigorously that through hard work, all things were possible.

"You could bring magic to this film," she said softly, a bittersweet ache in her chest. She knew how hard he'd worked and the sacrifices he'd made. An entire career dedicated to making movies, and he was still treated like a B-movie director. It wasn't right. Wasn't fair. "I would still love your help. Your schedule is open. Come work with me."

"No."

"Why not? This story could be your story."

"I'm not a cowboy."

Her lips pursed. He was being purposely obtuse. "You know what I mean—" Suddenly her voice broke. "You understand what it means to have a dream."

"So do you, my Eva, and this is your dream."

She hung up and buried her face in her hands, fighting tears, fighting exhaustion, fighting the desire to pick up the phone and call her father back and tell him all the things she wanted to say, like *I love you, Dad. I'm so proud of you, Dad.* But her father wasn't comfortable with expressing emotion. He wanted action, not words.

Lifting her head, she wiped a fist across her eyes. Her lashes were damp but there were no real tears. She didn't cry easily. She kept so much buried inside, and had ever since she was a little girl. She'd learned a painful lesson early on when she overheard the neighbors talking about her father, mocking his accent and what they perceived as eccentric behavior. Because they didn't understand him, they didn't like him.

She'd never forgotten that, and as she faced the biggest challenge in her career, she knew that no matter what happened on the film set, she had to fit in with the others. Her cast and crew had to be able to identify with her. They had to come first.

Rising from the bed, Eve went to the window, pushed back the drape and gazed out at the purple-black sky.

From the start, power plays between actors and directors had troubled the film, the fighting escalating until the entire cast and crew were sucked in. Now it was time to pull everyone together, to make them a team again. She could do it, too. She knew what they wanted—the same thing she did.

A great film.

Awards, bigger paychecks, accolades.

Tomorrow morning they were starting over. Tomorrow morning they had a chance to get it right. She'd be there in the thick of it with them. She'd be pulling for them, working beside them, proving that her cast and crew were the best.

And they were the best. She knew it in her heart. Now she just had to make them believe it.

Eve let the curtain fall. Tomorrow was the start of something big.

CHAPTER THREE

WHAT THE HELL HAD HE been thinking?

Zane gave up all pretense of sleeping and flung the covers back, sitting up in bed. He dragged an unsteady hand through his hair, wondering what had gotten into him at Carmen's. If he'd been drinking, he could blame it on the alcohol, but he'd been sober as hell.

He got to his feet, grabbed his jeans from the chest of drawers and stepped into them. Zipping his fly, he glanced at the bedside clock. Four thirty-three. They'd be here in four hours. He couldn't even imagine the chaos.

It'd kill him to watch a bunch of strangers take over his place…cars parked haphazardly, people streaming in and out, noise everywhere. Just like it had been after Jen's funeral. Everyone had come back here then, too, and the emotion and confusion had been overwhelming. Too much sorrow, too much loss, too many tears.

After pulling on a T-shirt, Zane headed for the bathroom. He turned the faucet on and didn't wait for the water to warm before splashing his face. The chilly water was a shock to his system. Lifting his head, he caught his reflection in the mirror. A day's growth of beard shadowed his jaw and chin. Hollows formed beneath his cheekbones and his dark green eyes looked bloodshot, as though he'd been up all night.

He had been up all night.

Zane dragged a sage-green hand towel over his face, his beard rasping at the cotton, and squeezed his eyes tightly shut. He had to find a way through this, had to find a way around the pain. Everybody said time healed all wounds, but so far time was only making it harder, only making it hurt more. He'd never meet another Jenny. He'd never love anyone the way he loved her.

In the kitchen he made a pot of coffee and was just about to pop bread into the toaster when Honey Bear padded in.

The blond Lab yawned and flopped down at Zane's feet. Zane smiled wanly. "I got you up too early, didn't I?" he said, leaning over to scratch the dog's ears.

Honey Bear had been a fluffy apricot-colored puppy when Zane gave her to Jen for their first wedding anniversary. He'd given her the dog for protection, and the two became inseparable immediately.

Honey had been beside herself when Jen died. For the first year and a half after the funeral, the dog set off, looking for her. Sometimes Honey would be gone for days on long, futile searches into the hills, and then back toward town. Once, a shelter in Reno called to say they'd found the dog. Another time a rancher outside Carson City drove Honey back.

It wasn't until two years passed that Honey finally gave up searching, but she never gave up waiting for Jenny. She still slept by Jen's side of the bed, and still waited at the back door every night just in case Jenny came home.

Just in case.

Zane swallowed roughly, hating the lump that filled his throat, hating the ache inside his chest that never seemed to go away. He poured a cup of coffee and took a scalding swallow. The coffee was strong. Good. It'd wake him up, force him to focus on the work that needed to be done and take his thoughts off all that would never be.

A few minutes later he grabbed his hat and made his way outside. Maybe, he thought with a tight twist of his lips, the chaos of the film was just what he needed.

When Eve and the caravan of cars, trucks and Winnebagos arrived at the ranch four hours later, Zane was nowhere around. Instead, J.T., one of Zane's longtime hired hands, appeared at the gate to welcome the stream of vehicles onto the property and show them where to park.

It was J.T. who walked Eve and her crew around the place, pointing out the electrical outlets, the bathrooms in the old bunkhouse, discovering what horses Eve wanted and when she'd need them.

The tour ended back where it began, in front of the corral, and Eve dug her fingers into the pockets of her black jeans, wondering at the butterflies in her stomach. The sudden fit of nerves made her feel more like sixteen than thirty-five, and briefly she wondered if her nerves had anything to do with Zane Dumas. No. Ridiculous. But she couldn't resist asking about him. "Did Mr. Dumas head into town?"

J.T. hesitated, looking awkward. "Guess you could say that."

Hmm, not a very convincing answer, she thought.

So Zane Dumas was avoiding her. Eve ought to be reassured, but somehow the rangy property seemed empty without him.

The big Dumas spread known as the Twin Bar Ranch had been divided between the Dumas kids, and the brothers had bought out their sister Melinda's share. Zach Dumas owned the front half, while Zane owned the rugged land butting up against the arid foothills. Having met Zane, Eve wasn't at all surprised at the way the property had been split. Of course Zane Dumas would want the rugged land and scrubby foothills; he wasn't exactly a people person, and the more isolated location was perfect for raising the skittish Arabians. "Will Mr. Dumas be back anytime soon?"

J.T. scratched his head. He couldn't have looked much more miserable. "Hard to say."

She bet it was.

Eve glanced over at the big trucks, knowing it would take at least an hour to unload and position the bulky camera equipment. "Well, tell him hello when you see him, and give him my thanks."

ZANE DID HIS BEST to keep his distance that first day. He worked in the stallion barn, then saddled up his horse and rode out into the hills, where he ate his lunch facing the small creek running across the edge of his rugged property. Sitting beneath a twisted oak tree under a vast blue sky, he could almost pretend that life was normal. He had the land. He had his work. He had pretty much everything he needed right here.

But his equanimity disappeared once he returned to the barn. As he rode up, he spotted crew members clustered around the yard, the men and women dressed casually in faded sweatshirts and unzipped windbreakers. He caught a glimpse of Eve standing at the edge of the corral, talking earnestly with an older, bearded man.

In her white cotton men's shirt and black jeans, she looked crisp and cool, and as she lifted an arm, pointing to the corral, the fabric of her shirt tightened, revealing the full shape of her breast. Zane sucked in a breath, his body hardening. She might look crisp and cool, but she made him feel hot. Hot, hard and hungry.

Swallowing, he steered his horse around and headed for the barn. Damn. She was making him *feel,* and this was going to be a problem. He didn't trust himself, and he certainly didn't trust his emotions. Emotions clouded one's thinking. Emotions meant mistakes.

The next morning, Zane made a point of finding work even farther from the corral, heading out in his truck to make a hay run, which would rule out the possibility of accidentally watching Eve work. Or Eve walk. Or talk. Or flash those blue eyes in his direction.

Just remembering her fiery blue eyes made something inside him tighten up. He craved contact with her, and that really scared the hell out of him.

Zane returned to the ranch at noon and parked behind the house. Honey bounded out of the truck, ears alert. As he stepped out of the truck, Zane stopped short, too, hearing raised voices coming from one of the Winnebagos lined up next to the old stone bunkhouse.

"What do you mean, you don't ride?"

Zane recognized Eve's voice and slowly shut the truck door and pocketed his keys.

"You *have* to ride, Ty," she continued shortly, exasperation evident in her voice. "You're a cowboy in a western. Riding isn't an option."

"You heard me. I *don't* ride."

Zane didn't want to hear more. This was exactly the kind of thing he wanted to avoid. But before he could escape, he heard this Ty-whoever-he-was add, "Just because I stretched the truth—"

"You didn't stretch the truth. You lied."

"What's the big deal? I wasn't cast because I'm a goat-roper. I was cast because I get people to the theater. Folks don't care if I can ride or not—"

"But I do," she interrupted. "And we're not paying you five million to let a stunt double do all your work. You're going to have to learn to ride—"

"No way. I don't like horses."

"Why?"

Brief silence. "Had a bad experience."

"Tough. You're not getting paid to take your shirt off. This is a western. You're a cowboy. You've got to get over your fear."

"Well—" the actor's voice dropped, his tone turning low and husky "—I suppose you could coach me a little...."

Eve groaned, and Zane could picture her expression. Her blue eyes would be snapping fire, her head would be thrown back, those amazing lips firmed in a straight line. But picturing her blue eyes and soft lips made him ache inside. This was stupid. *He* was stupid.

Disgusted with himself, he shook his head. What on earth was wrong with him? She was a *woman*. He didn't need another woman. He'd had his share of heartache.

His stride long and impatient, Zane headed toward the barn, eyes fixed on the ground. Suddenly he slammed into another body, a much smaller, slighter body, and before he could catch her, he sent Eve tumbling down.

Eve hadn't seen him. She was so angry she hadn't seen anything, and the impact shocked her, knocking the air from her lungs. Instinctively she threw her hands out, trying to break her fall, but it did no good. The gravel in the driveway chewed up her hands and gouged her knees.

"Are you hurt?" a voice asked from above her.

She felt a whisper of a shiver race down her spine. Zane Dumas. She could never forget his voice. The deep, husky timbre stirred something inside her, and she realized he didn't just have shadows in his eyes, but shadows in his voice.

Trying not to wince, she got back on her feet. "I'm fine," she said quickly, even though her knee was already throbbing and her palms were scraped raw. But her banged-up knee didn't hurt half as much as her pride.

"You're bleeding," he protested gruffly, reaching for her hand and ignoring her attempts to pull away.

"It's just a little cut."

"And even little cuts get infected."

"This one won't."

He looked at her hard. "You have a medical degree?"

She should have resented his tone, but she couldn't really hear his words, or his voice, not when he was staring at her that way. Her nerves were on edge, and her stomach did a peculiar flip.

He made her feel small, and fragile...vulnerable. But Eve wasn't comfortable feeling vulnerable. In fact, she hated it.

"No," she answered sharply, trying to jerk her hand free, but he held it too securely. "Just a physics degree."

"Physics?" he repeated, curiosity and disbelief tingeing his voice.

"Physics," she repeated smartly, hating how self-conscious she suddenly felt. Zane Dumas wasn't like any man she'd ever met before, and that was a good thing. Men in Hollywood were all about games. Zane Dumas didn't strike her as a game player.

"Is physics a requisite for film directors?"

Now there was a hint of laughter in his voice. She felt herself warm on the inside. He was having some effect on her. "It was a requisite for my dad. He wanted me to have a real job."

"He doesn't approve of making movies?"

Eve finally succeeded in pulling her hand from his. "It wasn't his first choice for me, but he's all right with it now."

Zane's dark eyebrows furrowed. He stared down at her for a long moment, and she could have sworn there was more he wanted to say, more he wanted to know, but he held back. "You better take care of that hand," he said after a tense silence.

"I will." She gave him her cool, professional smile, the one she reserved for tough business transactions, and sleazy producers who offered financial support for a little private TLC. She'd never gone that route, never played the casting couch game, and never would. "I promise to get my hand looked at later, if that'll make you feel better."

His expression was steely. "It won't make me feel better if you wait. Do it now. I have iodine in the house."

"Mr. Dumas—"

"Zane. You're going to be here awhile, you better use my name."

He sounded almost savage, and yet moments ago his touch had been gentle. There was something here, some strange energy between them. An awareness. A tension.

Chemistry.

Physics.

Newton's laws of motion.

Eve felt almost dizzy as she turned away, bracing her wounded hand to keep the blood from oozing onto her knit sweater.

Zane didn't like what was happening between them, either, she thought with sudden clarity as she gazed across the deserted corral. Her crew had scattered earlier when she and Ty went head-to-head, and now she was doing the same thing with Zane Dumas. But this wasn't business. It was personal.

And it had nothing to do with her scraped hand.

Zane Dumas felt the same energy she did. He was responding to the same uneasy momentum, and just like her, he was resisting it.

Her mind scrambled with old physics theories and laws, and she was reminded that science didn't apply in this case. A man and woman didn't answer to light, heat, energy, magnetism. A man and a woman weren't compelled by forces beyond their control. No, a man and woman could make choices, rational logical intelligent choices.

So why aren't you making any? she blasted silently. She couldn't afford any mistakes, and her response to Zane was frustrating the hell out of her.

She'd always liked strong men. She'd always liked successful men—men who knew what they wanted in bed and definitely had a level of expertise. But this attraction right now was altogether different. It felt hot and intense and primal. "I've got the crew waiting—"

"So send them to lunch." Zane stared down at her, green eyes flinty. "It's not as if you can continue filming. Your star's terrified of horses."

Eve froze. So he'd heard. The man seemed to know everything. "I can get a stunt double," she said defiantly. "I'll call L.A. and get someone here pronto."

"After you get that wound cleaned."

Furious words bubbled to the tip of her tongue, but with sudden clarity she realized that this was his place, his world, and if she wanted to get this film made, she'd have to work with him, not alienate him. "Fine," she said more quietly. "I'll let you wash the wound, but you're not using iodine. It stings."

They entered the long stone ranch house through a

side door, passed in and out of an old-fashioned mud-room before reaching a large, clean kitchen.

Everything looked immaculate. Spartan but immaculate. Right away Eve noticed the lack of feminine touches. There was nothing decorative in the kitchen, no photos, no knickknacks, not even canisters on the tile counters. But warm sunlight flooded the paned window above the sink, and the hardwood floor gleamed with a thick wax polish.

After directing Eve to take a seat at the table, Zane drew a first aid kit from one of the cupboards at the sink. Straddling a chair opposite her, he unscrewed a little black bottle. ''It won't hurt.''

She spotted the orange liquid a moment before he took her hand and swiped the cotton ball across her palm. ''I hate this stuff.''

''You're such a city girl.''

''I'm not—''

''You are, and I can't help wondering how you're going to get your star comfortable on a horse when you know nothing about riding?''

He had a good point, but he didn't realize she had a whole studio backing her. She had resources in L.A., experts at practically everything. ''I'm going to bring in a stunt coordinator—''

''Your actor seems to think you're going to give him a little coaching.''

Eve felt heat creep into her cheeks. So he'd heard that comment, too. She could cheerfully kill Ty right now. For that matter, she'd love to knock the self-righteous smirk off Zane's face, too, but she needed him a lot more than he needed her.

Glancing up at him, she noted the black T-shirt he was wearing, and the way it hugged his broad shoulders and well-muscled arms. He looked amazing. More like a film star than her five-million-dollar star.

Eve felt a quiver of desire as his fingertips trailed across her palm. An electric current surged through her and her belly exploded with warmth.

This was too much sensation. She hadn't felt this way in such a long time. Her hand trembled.

"Sorry," he said roughly. "Don't mean to hurt you."

"You're not."

Her voice sounded a little too high, a little too thin, and Zane abruptly lifted his head. He looked at her, and for one minute, neither spoke. Zane's eyes were the most beautiful sage green, flecked with bits of yellow and gray, and she let him look at her, into her, until the intensity was almost too much to bear.

In the back of her head Eve could hear one of her college professors lecturing, his voice flat, emotionless. *The study of chemical reactions that give rise to electric currents is, of course, electrochemistry.*

Of course. *He touches me and I feel a surge of electricity.* It was all chemistry. The ions, the chemical reaction, the transfer of energy.

Man, woman, touch, heat, pleasure, passion.

What would it be like to be with this man? What would it feel like to be in his arms…or beneath the hard length of his body?

Eve swallowed, almost panicked by the direction her thoughts were taking her. She couldn't lose focus. She couldn't afford to be attracted to Zane Dumas, especially now, when she had so much pressure riding on her. She had a job to do. She was behind schedule. She had an overpaid actor terrified of horses.

She swallowed again, her heart thudding, her mouth as dry as cotton. "I'd kill for a glass of water."

"Need any aspirin?"

"No, I'm all right."

He finished wrapping her palm with strips of gauze. "Keep it clean and you shouldn't have any problems."

Eve sagged in her chair as Zane moved away, heading to the sink to wash his hands before putting away the first aid kit.

She was exhausted. Wrung out. And all he'd done was patch up her hand.

Zane returned to the table and handed her the glass of cold water. "If you want to make that call, there's a phone behind you on the wall."

"Thanks, but I'll use my cell."

"We don't get great coverage out here. But it's your call."

She unclipped her cell phone from her belt and tried to dial out. He was right. Her phone couldn't find a strong signal.

Zane had left the kitchen when she unclipped her phone. He heard her shout to him a minute later, asking if she could use his phone, after all.

He almost smiled. She hated getting advice.

"Go ahead," he answered, and walked into the living room.

He heard Eve ask for a Bob Merrick as he looked out the living room window at the cluster of ranch buildings in the distance. Large white canvas tents had been rigged behind the buildings, and he could see the tops of the tents and the ruby-red roof of one of the semitrucks. Trucks, tents and phone calls to a Hollywood talent agency. What in God's name was happening to his life?

But the commotion of the film crew was nothing compared with the fire he felt when he touched Eve Caffrey.

She was waking something inside him and the emotion was strong. Too strong.

He didn't even have to touch her to want her. Was aware of her without looking at her. And when he did look at her...

He shook his head slowly. Eve had him thinking dangerous thoughts, thoughts that had nothing to do with horses, ranching or making movies.

No, what he wanted was much more private, much more personal, thoughts he hadn't had in years, needs he hadn't felt since Jen died.

He heard Eve hang the phone up, and then the echo of her footsteps in the hall. She appeared in the living room doorway, blond hair gleaming. "Good news, bad news," she said, smiling ruefully and running a hand through the thick golden strands.

With her hair lit up like sunshine and her mouth twisted in a wry smile, he was suddenly struck by her resemblance to Jen.

High cheekbones, full mouth, tousled blond hair.

Jen. Eve looked like Jen. Zane's gut tightened with shock and pain. That's why Zach had stared at Eve that night at Carmen's. That's why Eve was making him feel things. Jen was a darker blond than Eve, but they were both tall and slender and had the same lush mouth.

He wasn't attracted to Eve, but to the memory of his wife. He wasn't responding to Eve, but to the similarities between them. It wasn't Eve he wanted. It was Jen.

And just like that, all the things he missed about married life came rushing back.

He missed sitting on the front porch, watching the sunrise. He missed stretching out on the sofa together, listening to the evening news. He missed bumping a soft hip as they brushed their teeth before climbing into bed.

He missed climbing into bed.

Making love.

Falling asleep with the person you loved curled up against your ribs, beneath your heart.

Zane blinked. His chest was so hot it felt as though a fire raged inside of him. "What's the good news?" he rasped, barely holding himself together.

She looked at him, then away. "I can get a stuntman."

That was good news, Zane thought. "So what's the bad news?"

"I've got to wait almost a week for him."

That was bad news. One more week for Eve Caffrey to be in his life.

CHAPTER FOUR

TY WAS GOING TO BE an even bigger problem than she'd expected, Eve thought as they wrapped up a short, inconsequential scene that would probably end up on the cutting-room floor.

The film's star not only couldn't ride, but wouldn't try, and the fact he'd lied about it made Eve see red.

She was also furious with herself for not recognizing his fear yesterday. Ever since they'd arrived at Twin Bar Ranch yesterday morning, Ty had avoided the horses, going so far as to suggest scenes be restaged.

Such as sitting on the corral rail instead of the gelding. And cleaning the mud from his boots instead of the horse's hooves.

Grimacing, she closed her eyes and pictured a western film made without one shot of a horse.

"You wanted to see me, gorgeous?" The accent was Australian, the drawl pure Ty Thomas charm.

Australia's hottest export and Hollywood's sexiest new romantic lead had captured the world's imagination. With tawny hair, a rugged jaw and piercing blue eyes, Ty was good-looking without being too pretty, and was one of those rare actors who could play tough-guy roles without losing the women in the audience.

Yet right now he had a big problem with credibility.

No wonder the crew was up in arms. Ty was earning five million for this film and he wasn't performing. She couldn't fire him, either. That wasn't an option. The producers had made it clear that the only way this film would get funded was if Ty Thomas played the title role, and even more ironic was that Ty had been the one to request Eve as director.

"I do want to see you," she answered, lifting a hand in a quick farewell as one of the cars filled with crew members departed for the night.

"Is there a problem?" he asked, hauling himself up onto the corral railing.

He was seated above her now, and she had to crane her head back to see his face. The late-afternoon light played across his features perfectly—something she was sure he knew. Ty hadn't gotten where he was by chance.

But the conversation she needed to have with him wouldn't work this way. This wasn't about personality or charm, this was business. "Let's head to the bunkhouse. The catering truck left an ice chest with cold sodas on the steps. We can get something to drink and talk in the shade."

They reached the old stone bunkhouse and Eve took a seat on the front steps, her long legs braced in front of her. "Sit down, Ty. This might take a while."

He shot her a quizzical glance and dropped down next to her, his lean frame almost graceful. "What's on your mind, beautiful?"

As if she rivaled a Hollywood starlet. Eve's lips curved in a droll smile at the irony of it all. "I think you know."

He laughed once, the sound delightfully husky. "If it's about the movie—"

"Of course it's about the movie. The movie is why we're here." She shot him a swift glance. "As much as I like you, and as grateful as I am that you wanted me to take over this project, we've got a problem if you can't ride a horse."

"Eve—"

"No. Hear me out. You have to ride a horse in this movie. The script has you on or near a horse in sixteen scenes. We can't make this movie without you getting on a horse. Now, I'm going to give you a choice. You can decide to stick around here, learn the fundamentals of riding, or let me call Tim Walton and tell him this movie can't be made."

Ty didn't immediately answer. He leaned back, his white T-shirt rolled up high on his muscular arms, the cotton fabric still damp, misted by the wardrobe designer's diligent application of the water spray bottle. "You don't want to do that."

"But I'll have to if you can't carry this film. No stunt double can completely replace you. There are too many close-up shots, too many angles where the camera needs the real Ty Thomas in the frame.

He cocked his head, a dimple flashing in the lean plane of his cheek. He knew he had a killer smile. "You need this film. You need me."

Ty knew she'd been an assistant director forever, and as a woman, that put her pretty low on the totem pole. He also knew she was hungry for a bona fide success of her own.

All it would take was one big blockbuster and her star would rise.

"Yeah," she answered coolly, "I do need the film. You've worked with me on a couple of productions now and you know I'm tired of being treated like the coffee girl.''

She held his gaze a long minute, refusing to show an ounce of self-doubt. ''But I tell you what. I'd rather spend the next ten years running to Starbucks for lattes than put my name on a crummy film and have everyone think this was the best I can do.'' Eve drew a breath. ''Because I can do better. And so can you.''

Ty's features momentarily darkened and he turned his head away, giving her a glimpse of the profile that made women between the ages of sixteen and sixty swoon. ''I'm doing the best I can.''

''Are you? Is the partying really helping? Are the young girls improving your focus?''

When he didn't look at her, Eve felt a sudden pang. She had to tread carefully here. Actors were notoriously fragile, and Ty more explosive than most. If she wanted to persuade him to change, she'd have to prove she was on his side. That she believed in him. ''You're a brilliant actor, Ty. You've more talent than any other young actor I've worked with. You *can* learn to ride a horse.''

His features tensed. ''I'm not a coward.''

''I never said you were.''

''I am Jack Henry,'' he stated almost bitterly. ''I know this man. I understand him.''

''Then take some riding lessons. Let's get you over this fear of horses and make a great film.''

Ty sighed and braced his arms against his knees. A little over six-one, he was in excellent shape, his lean, muscular body honed to near perfection, his skin bronzed. ''I'll take the lessons, but I want a closed set. I don't want anyone around—except you, of course— and I don't want some big-name instructor from Hollywood who's going to make everyone curious. I want this private. I want it kept quiet. It'd ruin my reputation if word got out that Ty Thomas was afraid of horses.''

Not the movie. Not her career. Just his reputation. ''The studio is going to pressure me into hiring union—''

''Tell them no. In fact, don't tell them at all. This is between you and me. Find someone local, someone who won't talk. Because if this leaks out to the press…'' He let his voice drift off, not bothering to finish the sentence.

But then, he didn't have to. Eve already knew their production had fueled more gossip than almost any other film in years. She also knew there were plenty of people in Hollywood who'd be thrilled if she failed. She'd heard the rumblings in town before she left for Reno. A woman direct a western? Impossible.

Eve was determined to prove them wrong.

She also knew that if anyone could help her find an expert riding instructor for Ty, it would be Zane.

She spotted him heading for the front steps to the ranch house. Shadows stretched across the plain front yard, the entry nothing more than the long, low steps and a covered overhang.

Her shoes kicked gravel as she hurried over to him, and he turned on the porch to look at her. He'd showered and changed. Combed his hair a little bit differently, too.

''Do you have a minute?'' she asked, remaining on the walkway.

''Sure.''

Eve shifted her weight from one foot to the other. She might as well just ask him. The worst he could do was say no. "I need a riding instructor. Someone really good. Someone very discreet. Ty's agreed to take some lessons, but we've got to start tomorrow."

Zane frowned. "Lessons for what?"

"The movie. Ty Thomas. He's afraid of horses, remember?"

Suddenly he laughed and Eve blinked. She'd never heard Zane laugh, and Zane already knew that Ty couldn't ride.

This couldn't be Zane. This was the brother, the twin. Zach. "You're not Zane."

"No." Zach's eyes warmed, humor lurking in the sage-green depths. He came down the steps, stretched out a hand. "Zachary Dumas. Zane's baby brother here to check the plumbing in the bunkhouse."

Eve took in his expansive shoulders and firm bicep. "You don't look much like a baby brother."

"Well, I am. I was born fifteen minutes after the big guy."

She grinned despite herself. He was warm and funny. Definitely delightful. She put her hand into his and shook it. "Eve Caffrey. I'm directing a movie—"

"I know. *American Jack.*"

He released her hand, and Eve realized that while Zach had a strong, firm grip, she felt absolutely nothing when she touched him. So unlike the reaction she had when she touched Zane. "You know about the movie."

"I read the book." He crossed his arms over his chest and gazed down at her. For a moment he looked exactly like Zane, and then he smiled, and they were two different people again.

Zach's smile was all ease and warmth, but Zane's

smile was small, cynical, and failed to reach his eyes. No, the only thing in Zane's eyes was bitterness.

Bitterness and grief.

"You know the story, then?" she said, forcing her mind off Zane and back to business.

"Yeah. Zane's read it, too. Actually, he read it first and then passed the book on to me. Great story. Hope the movie's half as good."

Not much pressure there. But her thoughts had already moved on. So Zane had read the book. When she was pitching her cause—explaining her passion for *American Jack*—he already knew the story. He hadn't told her, though. He hadn't said much of anything. He'd just let her ramble on. "Your brother didn't tell me he'd read the book."

"Zane's not real expressive, is he?"

Her eyebrows shot up. "Talk about understatement."

Zachary's smile faded and he turned his head away. For a long moment he didn't speak. His narrowed gaze swept the distant corral and farm buildings and then he let out a slow, weary sigh. "Zane's been to hell and back. He's not easy to get to know, but he's still a great guy. When the chips are down, he's the one you want on your side."

The emotion in his voice touched her. "What happened?"

He took off his hat and ruffled his hair, which was streaked with glints of sun. "I really can't talk about it, but there was a terrible accident about five years ago." He shook his head, unwilling to say more. "Zane's never gotten over it."

A terrible accident five years ago, Eve repeated silently. What kind of accident had it been? Was Zane injured?

She tried to picture the kind of injury that would change a man so much. All kinds of lurid possibilites came to mind—broken bones, brain damage, spinal cord injury, crutches and wheelchairs.

Or maybe he wasn't the one hurt. Maybe he'd hurt someone else.

She didn't know the story yet, but she knew she had to find out. "I like him," she said softly, and it was true. He wasn't your average West Coast guy. Eve looked away and spotted Zane's Labrador heading for the stable. That's probably where Zane was now.

"As I said, he's not easy to get to know, but he's a good guy. He's one of the best." Zach pressed his Stetson back on. "Anyway, about the movie—Zane's your man. No one knows horses like Zane does. No one has a better touch. That's what made him so successful on the circuit."

"He competed?"

"He was good. If it hadn't been for Jen—" Zach broke off, anger shadowing his face. "Anyway, talk to Zane. He's your man." He nodded, tipped his hat and set off toward the bunkhouse with his leather satchel of tools.

Eve didn't immediately approach Zane. She needed to formulate a plan. If she didn't have a good argument when she asked for his help, he'd refuse her outright. She'd already learned that much about him.

But if Zach believed that Zane was the right man for the job, she believed him. These Dumas men weren't pushovers. They were smart, tough, hard-driving. They were also damn successful.

She could use a little success right now, too.

After mulling it over some more, she realized that Zane was exactly what she—and Ty—needed. Real riding expertise. Strength. Swagger. And confidence.

Eve downed the rest of her water and headed for the stable, where she found Zane raking hay.

She'd barely gotten through the first part of her request when he cut her off. "No" was his flat response. He stalked through the stable, entering a second stall. "Not interested."

Eve stepped around the small heap of hay, wan sunlight streaming through the high, narrow windows. "Come on, Zane. Just hear me out."

"I heard what you just said and I heard what you just asked. You want me to teach Thomas how to ride, and I said no."

Tiny bits of straw and hay flew into the air, forming pale clouds around them. Eve blinked, eyes stinging. "Why?"

"Because I don't like him."

She nearly smiled. Zane was a pain in the rear end, but at least he was honest. "You don't have to like him. You just have to teach him the fundamentals."

"Can't. I'm short on time—"

"It wouldn't take more than a couple days."

He made an impatient sound. "You're lucky I'm even letting you film here."

She stepped in front of him and grinned, going for cheerful and cute since practical wasn't working. "I am lucky. I'm really lucky, and I'd be even luckier if you worked with Ty."

"I'd rather let wild horses drag me through the brush."

"He's not that bad!"

Zane snorted. "He's a liar."

She shrugged. "He's an actor."

"The lack of morals doesn't bother you?" he challenged.

"I don't have time to judge. I've got a film that's falling apart and I need a riding instructor. I need someone really good."

"I'm not that good."

"Zach said you were."

Zane stopped raking, leaned on the handle and looked at her hard. "Zach?"

She batted a flying stalk of hay from the air. "He said you knew horses better than anyone around here. He said you used to compete on the circuit—"

"Zach talks too much," Zane interrupted curtly.

Eve scratched her nape. She must have gotten some hay down the back of her shirt. "He cares a lot about you."

"If he really cared, he'd mind his own business," he shot back, before raking again with short, angry jabs that created more dust than anything. "When did you see him?"

"Just a few minutes ago." Eve rubbed at her neck again.

"Well, he didn't say anything to me about it, and even if I wanted to do it, I can't. I'm short-staffed. I couldn't take a few days off for training. I don't have enough help around the place as it is."

"I'd pay you well. More than enough to allow you to hire extra help."

"This isn't about money!"

"Then what's it about?" she shouted back as she ran her hand up and down her neck.

He tossed his rake aside, muttering something incoherent beneath his breath. "Come here."

"What?"

Sighing with exaggerated patience, Zane marched toward her and turned her around. "You're scratching like a stray with fleas."

Her lips parted in protest, but all sound died as he suddenly lifted the back of her sweater and swept his hand across her skin.

"Hay," he said, brushing her again, his fingertips trailing down her spine from her sensitive nape to the small of her back.

Eve closed her eyes, wondering how such a simple touch could feel so lovely. It amazed her that a man of his size and strength could have such a gentle touch.

"There, that should help." Zane was tugging her sweater back down, job finished.

She stared up at him, no voice anywhere in her. She'd lost all rational thought, too. Part of her knew she should thank him, and another part wanted to beg for more.

But she wasn't the only one not talking. Zane was looking down at her, eyes dark, a rare glimpse of emotion hidden there.

"Zane," she said, her voice uneven, her heart beating a little faster, a little harder.

He didn't answer. Nor did he move away.

Eve didn't know what she was doing, only that she had to do something, had to reach him somehow. Slowly, carefully, she stretched a hand out and touched his chest, just above his heart. She felt the warmth through his black T-shirt, felt the hard curve of muscle beneath smooth skin. He felt just the way he looked—hard, sexy, beautiful.

She wanted to be near him, wanted to feel him. She took another step, closing the distance between them.

Rising on tiptoe, she hesitated briefly, then leaned forward—

"There you are, gorgeous." It was Ty, appearing in the stable door. "Wondered what happened to you. Had to ask one of the hands to help hunt you down."

Eve and Zane simultaneously took jerky steps backward, making them look like guilty children.

"You found me," Eve said, her voice sounding strained. "Just talking to Mr. Dumas."

Mr. Dumas. Eve cringed inwardly. How fake was that?

Thankfully Ty didn't seem to notice. He was smiling, his famous lazy grin, the one that made America's heart flutter. "So, boss, you still planning on giving me a lift back into town in that chariot of yours?"

Eve felt both men's eyes rest on her. Chariot, right. Her rental car was obviously on its last legs. "Sure am," she answered. "Let me just gather up my things."

Zane watched Eve head off with Ty and his stomach knotted. He felt as if he'd swallowed a handful of stones.

What was it about her that made him feel this way? And why did he even care that she'd gone off with that bigmouthed Aussie actor?

He'd been telling himself that he was responding to her because she looked like Jenny, but that was a bunch of crock. He knew there was more to the attraction than blond hair and a soft mouth.

He liked Eve.

He wanted Eve.

Eve wasn't an option.

Heading for the house, Zane thought about her latest request and felt a wave of irritation when he remembered how she'd offered him more money. Money! As if he needed any.

No, money didn't even make his wish list. The ranch's Arabian breeding program had become more successful than his wildest dreams. In fact, the whole ranch itself had outgrown his dreams.

This was supposed to have been his and Jenny's place, and instead he was here alone, working alone, living alone. Frankly, he was ready for a change.

On the steps of his house, he pushed his hat back and gazed out over the land and outbuildings. Had he maybe outgrown the ranch, as well?

A wave of uneasiness washed over him, and he shook his head. No, impossible. This was home. This place had always been home. He'd been born here, raised here. He was just tired tonight and a little bit lonely. What he needed was a night out. Some company. He'd head into town and see what his sister Melinda and her kids were doing. God knows he'd rather be wrestling on the floor and tossing pillows at his hellion niece and nephew than eating one more frozen TV dinner by himself in front of sitcoms that never made him laugh.

CHAPTER FIVE

THE CAR GAVE OUT WITH a snort and a sputter nine miles outside the Twin Bar Ranch and twenty-three from Reno. Eve barely had time to get to the side of the road before the steering column locked up and the electrical panel shut down.

"What the hell?" Ty demanded, forehead wrinkling as he leaned forward to inspect the dash.

"My thoughts exactly," Eve answered tightly, a knot the size of New Hampshire twisting in her belly. This was not the place to break down. And this was definitely not the time of day to be stranded.

The sun was nearly hidden behind the fawn-colored hills, and they were parked haphazardly on the side of a highway deserted in both directions.

"We better call the hotel—get someone to send help fast," Ty said, checking his watch. "I've got plans tonight."

Eve was sure he did, and they probably involved girls barely out of high school. "Wish I could," she said. "Battery's dead. Needs to be charged."

"Damn."

She pushed back a fistful of hair, tired, nerves on edge. "What about your phone?"

"Left it at the hotel this morning. Didn't think I'd need it."

"Damn," she muttered, briefly leaning on the steering wheel before throwing the door open and climbing out.

If she was working on the movie from hell, she had to be driving the rental car from hell. Eve slammed the door behind her and marched toward the smoking, steaming hood. First the car's air conditioner had given out. Then the stereo. And now this...this... slipped radiator hose, or whatever it was.

The engine hissed as she approached the fender, and Eve caught a whiff of hot oil tainting the dry air. "Dragon," she muttered, barely able to restrain herself from giving the front tire a kick. "Beast. Garbage can."

Ty slid from the passenger seat and stood up, resting a hand on the car's powder-blue roof. "Careful, love. You don't want to touch that. It's hot."

Really? It would have felt good to let out a shout, one good, piercing cry of frustration, but Eve wouldn't give herself the pleasure. Instead she seethed, just like the boiling, roiling mess beneath the shiny blue paint job.

Why couldn't anything be easy? Was it too much to ask for one problem-free day?

"You know, love, this could be fate." Ty smiled disarmingly, a dimple flashing in his lean bronzed cheek. "You and me, alone all night beneath a sky full of stars."

In that case, it'd be a very long night, she thought irritably, pressing her hands to her hips and managing a smile that felt nothing short of plastic. "Pop the hood, would you?"

"Sweetheart, you don't want to burn yourself."

"I won't. Pop the hood, Ty." The plastic smile was slipping.

"Do you even know what you're looking for?"

"Yes."

"I'm not talking car washes."

Her smile was gone. "Neither am I. I got my first break in the business staging car crashes. I have a science background and I minored in mechanical engineering. The hood, Ty?"

Finally he did as she asked, pulling the lever by the steering column. Eve lifted the hood, bracing it up on the support bar. Heat rolled out at her in waves, and she almost gagged at the stench of burnt oil. This was no slipped radiator hose.

Ty fanned the air. "Whew. Stinks."

She ignored him, noting instead the oil around the engine block and the spray on the hood. Not good.

"Well, what's the prognosis?"

Eve looked up. "I'm pretty sure it's a cracked head gasket."

His blue eyes met hers, so innocent. "Which means?"

"We're not going anywhere."

For almost an hour they sat on the car trunk. Ty tried to make a romantic move, which Eve coolly rebuffed.

The sun slowly dropped, and the lavender twilight gave way to deep purple shadows. Reluctantly Eve moved inside the car, knowing she'd have to reject Ty's advances all over again.

"Not interested, Ty," she said, pressing him back with the tips of her fingers. "You and me—we're business, and only business."

"I'm just trying to keep you warm," he said, reaching around to rub her shoulder.

She peeled his hand from her. "I'm not cold." *Yet,* she mentally added.

It had been a long day, and right now it was looking like a very long night. Silently she stared up at the sky through the dusty windshield, watching as the first stars appeared, and the moon shone like a sliver of cream custard in the sky.

Close to seven-thirty, headlights gleamed on the horizon. Eve flung open her door and frantically attempted to flag down the passing motorist.

Luck was on their side. The driver slowed and then pulled over, kicking up dust and gravel. The truck's tinted window rolled down.

Eve's heart did a funny little two-step as she spotted a painfully familiar face. "Zane."

For a moment he said nothing. He just stared at her, taking in the car with the propped hood. "You've got to be kidding."

She struggled to smile, her cheeks stiff. She'd been so strong until now, so tough, but there was something about Zane that undid her, that made her feel so many conflicting emotions. "Wish I was."

With a silent shake of his head, Zane backed up and pulled in front of her car, his headlights illuminating the engine.

"Head gasket," Eve said wearily as Zane swung out of the truck cab. Together they stared into the yawning space beneath the rental car's hood. "At least I think it's the head gasket."

Zane leaned forward and swiped the moisture pooling on the engine block with the tip of one finger, then rubbed his fingers together. "Oil. You're probably right."

Ty stepped round the side of the car. "Your horses have these problems, mate?"

Zane looked as if he was just dying to give a sarcastic response, but he restrained himself and turned to Eve instead. "What happened to your cell phone?"

She touched her waist. "Battery's dead."

Thank God he didn't lecture her. He closed the car hood. "Grab your stuff. I'll give you a ride to town. You can call a tow truck from the hotel."

The inside of Zane's truck smelled of hay, leather and the spicy scent of his cologne. He must have just shaved, she thought, feeling his warmth and getting a glimpse of his hard, smooth jaw.

She was sitting in the front, sandwiched between Zane and Ty, and although she felt absolutely nothing when Ty's thigh brushed hers, she was acutely aware of Zane even without contact. She could feel him without a touch, want him without a glance. He just connected with a part of her that no one had ever connected with before.

Zane accelerated onto the highway. He drove the way a man should drive—fast, focused, controlled. He knew the road well and he knew his truck, and there was something about the way he carelessly rested one hand on the steering wheel and the other on the door that struck her as incredibly sexy.

But then everything about Zane was sexy.

She wasn't prepared when the truck hit a pothole and she bumped up against Zane. Reaching out instinctively her hand came into contact with his thigh, near his zipper, and she suddenly became very conscious that he was hard. Everywhere.

Her face heated. Her body warmed. She didn't want

to stare at his crotch, but the man did have an amazing lap. She wouldn't mind sitting there.

They hit a second bump and the truck bounced again, but this time Eve caught herself before she fell against him. "Sorry."

Zane growled something in the back of his throat and reached for the radio dial, turning it on. Static scratched from the speakers and he played with the dial again, his long arm inches from Eve's breast, his thigh practically touching hers.

She shot him a swift sideways glance. Being this close to him, her body tingled and she felt heat everywhere, heat and energy and waves of desire so strong that she pressed her knees together, aching inwardly for what she didn't have and might never know.

Unless she could convince Zane to spend some time with her, get to know her as a woman and not as a director. She had a feeling he didn't particularly go for high-powered females, not that she was high-powered. She was still trying to climb her way up.

His hand dropped from the radio to his thigh. She glanced down at his strong fingers. He was wearing faded jeans and a dark brown belt with a large silver buckle. Zach had said that Zane used to compete on the rodeo circuit, and Eve wondered if he'd earned that buckle. She couldn't imagine him buying one that big, otherwise.

"Is that buckle from a rodeo win?" she asked, gesturing to his waist.

His eyes never left the highway. "Yeah."

"You used to compete."

"A little."

The silver buckle was a thick oval, decorated with elaborate scrolls. "Zach said you were really good."

Zane's mouth flattened. "I got to keep you and Zach apart." He didn't smile, but he didn't sound angry.

"Why'd you give it up?" she persisted.

"There was a problem." When she didn't say anything, he reluctantly added, "An accident."

Ty suddenly looked interested. "Did you get hurt?"

Zane shot him a quelling glance. "That's one way of putting it," he said, bitterness edging his voice and stifling further discussion.

Ten minutes later Zane pulled in front of the hotel and parked beneath the navy-and-cream awning.

Before he'd even killed the engine, Ty opened the door, jumped out and extended a hand to Eve. "Thanks, mate," he drawled with a mocking two-finger salute. "See you round."

Eve flushed. Ty's insincerity was appalling. He needed a lesson in manners, but tonight wasn't the time, not when the production still lacked momentum.

"Thank you," she added firmly, trying to ignore the tension charging the air. "You saved us—"

"You didn't save me," Ty interrupted. "I was fine. We were fine."

She shrugged impatiently. "Since I can't speak for Ty, let me speak for myself. You saved *me,* and I appreciate it."

Zane shifted into neutral, and his foot eased off the accelerator. "My pleasure."

Something twisted in her chest, a knot of emotion she didn't understand. "Is that so?"

His sage-green eyes locked with hers and his smile faded. "Yeah."

For a moment neither spoke, and there was a sizzle of something between them, some current of energy...possibility, and then Ty cleared his throat. "Coming, Eve?"

She wanted to say no. She wanted Zane to give her a reason to say no, but he didn't say a word. "Yes," she said, and stepped back.

Ty slammed the door closed.

Zane pulled away and Ty headed toward the hotel's double glass doors. But Eve remained where she was on the flagstone entry, watching the truck near the exit.

Suddenly her control snapped. She didn't want him to go. Didn't want Zane to drive away. She had so much to do, and yet Zane was making rational thought impossible.

She sprinted forward and called his name, knowing that his window was rolled down.

The truck's brake lights flashed red. He'd stopped. Then the black truck gunned backward, pulling next to Eve. "What's up?"

He was leaning out his window and the air had ruffled his hair. He looked so damn sexy. Her heart gave a funny double thump. "I'm going to need a new rental car for the morning. I didn't know if you'd be willing to drive me to the rental agency now."

His eyes searched hers. "Maybe you have plans," she said, feeling less confident.

"I have time to take you."

She smiled. She couldn't help it. He just made her really happy. "Not to push my luck, because I know I'm already really *lucky* to be shooting the film on your ranch, but if you have time, could I take you to dinner?"

"Dinner."

"Yes, you know, food. I'd love to treat you."

"You're getting rather demanding, aren't you?"

He was teasing her. It was a huge step in the right direction. "So I've been told."

"Dinner sounds great, but I've got a condition. I get to pick the place."

"You do?"

Her quick response elicited another smile, and suddenly Zane looked just like Zach—relaxed, rugged, incredibly easygoing. "I do. You want to argue about that, too?"

She grinned. "No. Let me just get my paperwork and make a quick change."

It wasn't a date, she reminded herself as she took the elevator up to her room on the top floor of the hotel. It was just dinner. He was giving her a ride to the rental-car office and then they were going to dinner, and dinner was just a way to show her appreciation. But her racing heart was ignoring all attempts at rationalization, and truth be told, she felt disgustingly happy.

Guys didn't usually do this to her. She was too serious, too pragmatic for valentines and romance, yet right now, she felt positively giddy.

It was crazy, but she was so turned on.

Once in her room, Eve stripped off her shirt, rummaged through her closet and pulled a black silk blouse from a hanger. Quickly she slipped on the blouse, swapped belts and shoes, then combed her hair and touched up her makeup.

"Turned on" was an understatement, she thought as she headed for the elevators. She'd give just about anything to kiss the man.

He had to be a good kisser. She prayed he'd be a good kisser. Maybe tonight she'd find out.

Ty was waiting for her in the lobby. "I just called

your room," he said, falling into step beside her. He'd showered and changed, and there was a gaggle of young women with teased hair and lots of eye makeup following his progress across the lobby.

"Thought you might be heading to dinner," he said, flashing his famous smile. "Want some company?"

Eve shouldered her black purse. "I have plans," she said, not particularly wanting to elaborate. There was little love lost between Zane and Ty and she hoped to avoid any added conflict tonight.

They'd reached the front door and Ty glanced around the lobby, then outside. His gaze fell on the parked black truck. "You're going with *him?*"

"Zane's helping me with the rental car."

"He's a redneck."

"He's not." Eve didn't know why she was having this conversation with him. She was the boss—barely, a small voice challenged her—and Ty was ten years younger than her. Even if she wasn't directing the picture, she'd never go out with him. "I'll see you in the morning. Don't forget we've a 7:00 a.m. call."

He ignored her attempt to change the subject. "You're not just exchanging the car, are you."

She glanced out at the truck, saw that Zane had opened his door and was heading their way. "We might get some dinner, too. Zane has something in mind, but it's casual, nothing to get worried about."

"Everything okay?" Zane asked, shooting her a peculiar look as he met her in the driveway.

"Just fine," she answered, grateful when they reached his truck, leaving Ty behind. Thank goodness she wouldn't have to deal with him again until morning.

After picking up her new car, she followed Zane to

a country-western bar in a rustic building at the edge of town. McCornick and Weston's featured a live band, sawdust on the floor and strings of colored lights overhead. Eve had never particularly liked country music before, but for some reason, tonight it sounded easy on her ears and matched her mood.

They ordered the house speciality—steaks, barbecue ribs, garlic bread and salad—and then bottles of beer, although Zane asked for a nonalcoholic kind.

For a moment after the waitress left, neither said a thing. They just sat there in the small booth, breathing in the bar's fragrant smell of straw and barbecue sauce.

Eve couldn't stop looking at Zane. He was wearing a soft green V-neck sweater that revealed just a hint of curling golden brown hair. His skin looked so warm and smooth that she itched to reach out and touch him. Could he possibly feel as good as he looked?

It suddenly crossed Eve's mind that their worlds were so different. Here she was at thirty-five, finally making her first big-feature film. She'd never married, never had kids, never even owned her own home. Zane didn't just own a home, but a working ranch.

"How's the movie going?" he asked, leaning against the padded booth cushion.

"Fine."

"Any problems—other than a star who's afraid of horses?"

She smiled faintly and shook her head. "No. Things are…fine."

"You don't really want to talk about the movie, do you?"

She shrugged. "It's not that, it's just…"

"Work," he guessed.

"Exactly." Eve tucked a strand of hair behind her

ear. "Sometimes it takes over everything, if you know what I mean."

A bleak expression briefly appeared in his eyes. "I know what you mean."

Eve stared at him for a moment, feeling the strangest current of tension. She heard what he was saying, but she also felt his unease and sadness. He was a man with a past.

The band, which had taken a quick break, returned to the small stage and began playing a new set. The waitress arrived with their beer, the dark bottles tall, cold and beaded with condensation.

Zane smiled crookedly and lifted his nonalcoholic beer. "To your movie."

Eve shyly clinked bottles. "Thanks."

They both drank, then Zane set his bottle on the table. "About your request—"

The sound of an amplified fiddle drowned out the rest of what he was saying. Frowning in concentration, Eve leaned forward. "What did you say?"

"You needed an instructor—"

She shook her head, utterly bewildered. "Tractor?"

"Instructor—riding instructor," he shouted.

The fiddle just grew louder. "Riding a tractor?" Eve hollered back.

Zane grinned crookedly and gave his head a rueful shake. "Forget it." He pushed aside his bottle and leaned across the table. "Dance with me."

She wasn't hearing him right. *"What?"*

He slid from the booth, stepped toward her and reached for her hand. "Dance with me."

This time she didn't need words. His expression said everything. There was something fierce and alive in his eyes, an intensity she couldn't deny. Slowly she placed her hand in his. His fingers closed around hers, and a flicker of fire made her whole arm tingle from palm to shoulder.

Zane walked Eve onto the dance floor, his hips so close to hers she could feel his heat. Something was happening, she thought rather wildly as her heart beat faster and color flooded her cheeks.

He drew her closer into his arms. "Ever two-step before?" he asked, dipping his head, his breath warm against her ear.

His voice vibrated straight through her. Eve tipped her head back to look into his face, but all she could see was his outline against the glow of red and yellow lights strung overhead. "Once. A long time ago."

"Just follow me." His hand settled on her waist. "I'll teach you."

There was a rough caress in his voice that danced along her spine, and she shivered as his fingers curled against her side, the heat from his hand penetrating her black silk blouse. The way she was feeling, she doubted she could get her feet to obey.

He took a step toward her, into her, one hard thigh practically between her legs.

"I don't know if this is such a good idea," Eve choked, the chemistry between them almost overpowering. "I might make a fool of us."

"Impossible." His green eyes glinted. "I'm too good a dancer. Just stay close to me." And with that he took the lead, hips bracing hers, his chest grazing her breasts.

He was a good dancer. A great dancer. It amazed her that Zane was as comfortable on the sawdust-strewn dance floor as he was in the saddle. For such a muscular man, he had surprising grace…his steps so controlled they were almost fluid.

As they took a quick spin around the dance floor, her body supported by his, some of her anxiety began to ease. It was exhilarating, moving so fast. It was…fun.

"You're doing great," he mouthed against her ear, and a rush of pleasure shot through her. She loved the way he held her, loved the firm pressure on her waist, the strength in his body. She could feel his thighs against hers, the movement of his hips, and for a split second Eve wished she was naked, wished she could feel him against her bare skin.

Wished they'd make love.

For the next half hour they danced, dipped and twirled around the floor. Despite the fact that Zane was the biggest man on the dance floor, he was by far the best dancer, and by the time the last fast song finished, they were both breathless and laughing.

She tilted her head back. "That was amazing. You're amazing, Mr. Dumas."

He thrust a hand through his hair, pushing it off his forehead. "We're back to 'Mr. Dumas,' are we?"

"No. Not at all."

"Good. Because I was hoping you'd dance this next one with me." His green eyes darkened. "Think you can manage that?"

The band had changed tunes, slowing the tempo, and the look he gave her made the breath catch in her throat. There were shadows in his eyes, along with something else, something hot and bright and fierce.

"I think I can," she answered faintly.

He drew her back into his arms, and Eve liked the way he adjusted his stride to hers, liked the instinctive way he made them fit…legs, hips, shoulders. She felt herself relax, her cheek nestling against his chest.

The music seemed to wrap them snugly together, until they were hardly moving. Eve's lashes drifted closed, and she concentrated on the even thud of Zane's heart and the spicy fragrance of his skin. He was all man and he made her feel all woman—

"Can I have this dance," a deep Aussie voice drawled, followed by a not-so-gentle tap on Zane's shoulder. "Or are you going to monopolize the lady all night?"

CHAPTER SIX

EVE FELT ZANE'S POWERFUL frame stiffen.

She had a horrible vision of him throwing a punch in the middle of the crowded dance floor, and for a split second thought he'd really do it when he lifted a clenched hand.

"Zane." She applied pressure to his arm even as she faced Ty. "What are you doing here?"

"Came to hear the music," Ty answered, smiling a devil-may-care grin that put Eve's teeth on edge. She knew as well as he that this wasn't a chance meeting. Ty had tracked them down.

"Then listen with your ears, not your feet, and sit down," Zane retorted, jaw tight, eyes hard.

Ty's shoulders immediately squared. "Who're you talking to, mate?"

"You." Zane shook off Eve's restraining hand.

The only thing Eve could see was Ty's beautiful face all mashed up like a sweet potato, and God help them, that was the last thing she needed now. This couldn't happen. There couldn't be a fight. *"Zane. Don't."*

He wasn't listening. She could feel his fury wash over her in hot waves. He was dying to throw a punch. He was just that kind of man. Intense. Physical. Territorial.

She moved between the men, using her body as a

shield, but that didn't let Ty off the hook. He had no business being here and she couldn't help wondering just how many restaurants he'd hit before he found her and Zane at McCornick and Weston's. "How'd you get here?"

The actor gestured behind him with a thumb. "Danny and some of the crew."

Danny O'Connell, her lighting whiz, was an irresponsible, party-loving soul if ever there was one. Danny and Ty had already been thrown out of one bar this week. Eve didn't want to make it two. "This isn't going to work, Ty."

"What?" he asked, his expression the picture of innocence. "I just came with the guys to hear the band. No reason to get hot and bothered."

"Then leave her alone," Zane said curtly, temper barely leashed. "She's your boss, not your girlfriend."

"Never said she was."

"Then give her some space—"

"What's your problem, mate? You don't even know her. You're just some redneck—"

Zane's right arm swung out to grab a fistful of Ty's shirt and pull him up close, trapping Eve in the middle. She felt like a pressed flower and knew there was no way in hell they'd get any filming done if Ty sported a black eye and split lip.

"Get your hands off him, Zane." Her voice sounded cold even to her own ears. "Now."

She couldn't read Zane's expression, but she could hear his breathing, deep and shallow. He was furious. "What about him?" Zane demanded.

People were watching. They'd begun to draw a crowd. Even the band had stopped playing.

From the corner of her eye, Eve could see the

bouncer heading their way. They were about to get tossed out. This was not how she wanted to get her name in the paper.

She turned and placed her hand on Zane's chest. His heart thudded wildly beneath her palm. "Let go of him. Now. I won't let you do this."

"You're taking his side," Zane shot back.

"I'm not taking sides. I just don't want a fight."

Zane hesitated, his body tense with leashed anger.

"Go on," Ty taunted Zane. "Run on home."

Eve could have happily slapped Ty upside the head for that one. Instead she shot him a scathing glance. "Knock it off, Ty. You don't need another story in the paper."

She wanted to say more, wanted to tell them they were both behaving like kids, but she knew whatever it was between them wouldn't be settled by her. From the very start they'd taken a deep dislike to each other.

Her problem was getting Ty out of the bar without a broken, bloody nose and a visit by the cops.

"Let him go, Zane," she repeated, hating herself, hating Ty, hating that the evening had to end this way, but work came first. This damn movie had to come first. And she knew Ty didn't have the control. If someone were going to back off, it would have to be Zane. "Zane, please let go. Walk away before this gets really nasty."

There was a long moment of strained silence before Zane slowly, resentfully released Ty. "If that's what you want."

Zane turned around and walked out without looking back.

Ty smoothed the front of his shirt as the door closed

behind Zane. "Chicken," he said. "He probably doesn't even know how to fight."

Eve's stomach cramped. Her head hurt. Her heart hurt. She hated her job right now. "Shut up, Ty."

If only she could have followed Zane out, explained to him, apologized—something. But there was no way she could risk leaving Ty alone. She didn't trust him. She'd worked with Ty before and he'd never been so unpredictable, or antagonistic, but for some reason this production was bringing out the worst in him.

"Have you been drinking?" she demanded.

"No. Well, just a beer. At the hotel. But that was a couple hours ago."

Eve stared at him, her insides cold. She didn't know what to think. Didn't know how she was going to get through the next four to six weeks with him.

Ty read her doubt and frustration. "Look, Eve, I'm sorry, okay? I was just playing around."

His apology didn't make her feel better. She liked Zane. She really liked him, and if Ty had screwed things up… Eve shook her head, not wanting to go there. "What I do in my private time is my business, Ty. We work together but we don't have a relationship. Got it?"

ZANE SAW RED. Seething, he drove as if he had the devil on his back, and even with the truck windows down and the wind rushing in his ears, he couldn't escape his fury.

Thomas was a fool. A cocky, overly confident pretty boy who'd get his butt kicked one of these days if he wasn't careful. And he almost did tonight.

But Zane was more furious with himself than Ty.

He hated losing control, and that's exactly what had

happened tonight. He'd made a complete ass out of himself. Acted like a Neanderthal.

Grimacing, he remembered just how close he'd come to dragging Thomas out of the bar for a little private conversation outside.

Zane felt disgusted and embarrassed. He hadn't gotten into a fistfight since he was a kid. So why had he lost it tonight?

Eve.

Eve was a temptress. He'd known it from the start, known that anyone built like she was, with a face like an angel and brain power, as well, would turn him inside out. She was doing just that and more. He might not go to church anymore, but Zane remembered what happened to the man who fell for Eve. Trouble, trouble, trouble.

And he was getting it in spades.

Jaw aching, muscles too tight, Zane drew a breath. What he wouldn't give to knock Ty Thomas down a peg or two. But he wouldn't. Thomas might be a spoiled little baby, but he was Eve's problem, and if Zane messed with Ty, he would be messing with Eve's movie. And Eve needed this movie bad.

Back home, he stripped and showered beneath cold, hard needles of water, but the icy blast did little to soften his desire. Even now, an hour after leaving the bar, he could still feel her. Could feel the warmth of her body and the softness of her skin and the way she fit against him. He wished his feelings could be put down to something chivalrous, but he wasn't feeling chivalrous. He was feeling possessive. Territorial. And there was nothing he could do about it. Nothing but keep his distance from Eve.

It had been a mistake to join her for dinner, and an

even bigger mistake to ask her to dance. But it wasn't too late to get some control.

Just because he was attracted to Eve didn't mean he had to act on it. There was no reason to be near her at all. She had her job. He had his. She could find someone else to teach Ty to ride, and he'd be damned if he put himself in close contact with her again.

Besides, he had a lot of other things to deal with. The ranch always needed work. Zach was going to be married before long. And then there was that whole matter of his parents not being his parents, which was as ridiculous a thing as he'd ever heard.

Babies weren't switched at birth. People didn't really do things like that. He was a Dumas. He had to be a Dumas. And if he wasn't, then who was he?

IT TOOK EVE A MOMENT to register that it was the phone ringing, not someone at her door.

Sitting up, she peered at her bedside clock and struggled to make out the time. One-thirty. "Hello?" she croaked, pushing tangled hair from her face.

"Eve. It's me. I'm still at McCornick's and I don't think I should be driving right now." Ty actually sounded a little embarrassed. "Can you send someone to pick me up, sweetheart? I'm waiting out front."

Eve heard someone else laugh, a girlish giggle, and her stomach tightened. Ty's weakness for pretty young women was one of the things that had led to blows between him and Hans Andersson, the film's last director. A perfectionist and an artist, Hans couldn't tolerate Ty's drinking or skirt chasing.

No wonder Hans got fed up, Eve thought, throwing the covers back and swinging her legs out of bed. Ty didn't know when to say "enough." "I'll be there in five minutes. Stay put. Don't go anywhere."

After seeing Ty to his room, Eve went back to bed, but she couldn't fall asleep.

If Ty hadn't come bursting onto the dance floor tonight at McCornick and Weston's, Eve was pretty sure she could have gotten Zane to agree to work with him. But after the scene at the bar, she knew it'd be a cold day in hell before Zane would give Ty lessons.

He probably wouldn't be too interested in speaking to her, either.

Eve closed her eyes, feeling really unprepared at the moment for the demands of this film.

She'd always wanted to make a big picture, but she'd imagined herself calm, cool, controlled—not scrambling from disaster to disaster, barely able to keep her head above water.

But she couldn't give up. She wouldn't give up. Her lifeboat might be peppered with holes, but Eve knew what she had to do and was determined to get it done.

THE NEXT MORNING, it took Eve a couple of phone calls, but she found a riding instructor willing to work Ty into her schedule if Ty could be at her ranch ASAP.

Ty wasn't thrilled about waking up early. Hungover and short-tempered from lack of sleep, he refused to climb into the car without breakfast and a second cup of coffee. He lingered over his coffee until Eve finally yanked the ceramic cup away and asked the waitress to pour the rest into a to-go cup.

"I don't want to do this," Ty muttered as Eve walked him to the waiting car.

"I don't care." Eve faced Ty, grateful that one of

her assistants was escorting Ty to his riding lesson this morning. Eve needed a break from Ty, and a chance to view the film dailies from yesterday. "It's not an option. We're running out of time, Ty."

Three hours later, Eve was sitting with the lighting and camera crew in the screening room they'd set up in the hotel banquet space, when she got a call from the assistant director.

"You might want to get down here," he said tersely. "I don't think Ty can do this."

"Why not?"

"He's been out here three hours and he still can't even bring himself to groom a horse."

"Groom a horse," Eve repeated woodenly, glancing at her watch. "You're telling me he's not even in the saddle yet?"

"No."

"He's still trying to brush the horse?"

"Yes."

Could this get any harder? "I'll be there as soon as I can."

She arrived just before noon and discovered Ty perched uneasily in the saddle. He gripped the reins with two hands, feet jammed tightly in the stirrups.

"That's great." Patti, the riding instructor, encouraged him as she held the horse at the bridle. "You're doing great."

Eve almost choked. *Great?* Ty was covered in a cold sweat, and his hands shook as he clenched the reins. You could put a man in a stable, she thought, but you couldn't make him like a horse.

"Let's see you trot around the corral," Eve said, ducking between the railings to step inside the ring.

Patti's red ponytail swung as she turned to face Eve. "Oh, he's not trotting yet."

"How about a nice easy walk, then?" Eve asked, trying to hang on to her temper. They didn't have time for this. Ty had to be riding, *really riding,* soon. Tomorrow. Friday at the latest.

"We're not quite there," Patti replied with a bright smile. "But Mr. Thomas is making excellent progress. Just look at his straight back and the way his hips sit in the saddle. He looks wonderful, doesn't he?"

No, he didn't look wonderful, he looked sick and sweaty and scared witless. Not exactly hero material. But Patti was beaming up at Ty, and Eve realized she had fallen under the actor's spell. This was disastrous. Ty needed boot camp, not a fan club.

Patti ended the lesson at four, when the first of her after-school lessons showed up. Ty climbed into Eve's car and stretched. "What do you think, boss? Did you see me on the trail ride? Pretty good, hey?"

The "trail" ride had been a lesiurely walk around Patti's farm and stable, but if Ty wanted to think of that as a trail, fine. More power to him. "I did see you."

"Patti says I'm a natural."

"You're definitely ready for the next step." Eve kept her gaze fixed out the windshield and tried to bite back the sarcasm. "Think you'll be ready to go for a longer ride tomorrow? You know, go a bit faster, try some different terrain?"

Ty wrinkled his straight nose. "I don't know. I feel good with what we did today. And you know, despite riding all day, I've still got energy to head out tonight." He tossed her a grin. "Want to go dancing?"

"*Ty.*"

"It's just dancing."

"No."

"You went dancing with that redneck—"

"Drop it." Her voice came out sharper than she'd intended, but they drove the rest of the way in blessed silence.

Hours later, Eve was woken once again by the insistent ring of the phone. It couldn't be, she whimpered, reaching for her pillow and clamping it over her head. Not another middle-of-the-night wake-up call. Not another problem.

What did Ty need now? Chinese takeout? A ride home from a club? A bottle of Johnny Walker Black?

Well, he could forget it. They could all forget it. She wasn't going to answer.

Eve pressed the pillow harder against her ears, elbows locked tight, telling herself eventually the caller would give up. The phone would stop ringing.

But it didn't stop.

She waited nearly one full minute and it just rang and rang and rang.

What the hell was the matter with him? Did he really think he was the sun and the moon and the center of the universe? Groaning, she threw the pillow off her head and lunged for the phone. "Yes?"

It was Ty. And the situation was worse than she imagined.

Eve dressed in less than sixty seconds, tossing on clothes and grabbing her wallet.

Damn it. If Ty wasn't such a box office success, she'd have him drawn and quartered. Immediately.

The Reno jail looked just like every other city jail— square, squat, narrow windows. The downtown core was deserted at four in the morning, and Eve parked on the street and pocketed her keys.

It took a while to handle all the paperwork and arrange for bail. The drunken brawl Ty had been involved in at McCornick and Weston's had resulted in considerable property damage. When he was finally released, Eve turned around and walked out the front door without a word to him.

Her arms were tightly folded across her chest and her heart hammered painfully hard. She was furious.

When they reached the car, Eve unlocked the doors and tossed her purse onto the front seat.

"Eve—" Ty said, hesitating.

She shook her head. She couldn't do this right now. Didn't he get it? This movie was a big deal, a huge deal, and she couldn't bear to stand by and watch him screw it up. "Get in."

"I'm sorry."

Not as sorry as he was going to be.

Ty dozed as she drove. It was almost five, and the purple sky was fading to blue. Ty would be nursing one miserable hangover next time he opened his eyes.

He did open his eyes, briefly, when she shifted into Park. "We're here?" he asked, yawning and turning his head against the leather headrest.

"Depends where 'here' is," she said, staring out the window at the low stone house with the long wood veranda. Lights shone from one window, which meant Zane must be up.

With a sigh, Ty snuggled deeper into the seat. "A couple eggs, sunny-side up, gorgeous. And ham steak. Grilled."

Eve clamped her jaw tight and got out of the car.

She climbed the three steps to the house and reached up to knock on the door.

Her hand hovered in midair, and for a split second she questioned her sanity. Just what was she doing here? Why did she think Zane would—could—help?

She didn't have to wait long to find out. From inside the house she heard Honey barking and then the hall light switched on. The door opened and Zane stood there, barefoot, wearing just jeans and white T-shirt, coffee cup in hand.

He stared at her for a moment, then lifted his cup to his mouth and took a sip. "You look like hell."

"It's been a long night."

Zane inclined his head. "Heard your hero got a taste of our local jail." He caught her surprised expression. "It was on the late news. It'll probably be in the morning paper, too."

"Great." Eve dug her hands into her jeans pockets. Wait until the producers read about this. She'd be lucky to keep her job through the weekend.

Zane's expression softened. "Is every film this tough?"

"Movies are never easy. Something usually goes wrong. Difficult actor, bad script, problems with the crew. Even food poisoning. But this…this takes the cake."

"You ever think about another line of work?"

"No." No hesitation there. Eve loved the business. Loved the creativity and the challenge. Loved juggling the massive scope of such a project against the gazillion tiny details.

"I take it he's sleeping it off now?"

She glanced behind her at the new rental car. It was a white luxury sedan. The kind with plush leather seats the color of caramel, and endless legroom front and back. "You could say that."

How exactly was she supposed to segue to the next part? How to throw herself on Zane's mercy and beg for help? "He's passed out."

Zane took a step past her, walking to the edge of the veranda and looking out at the car. Ty's profile was visible through the windshield, his head tipped back, lips parted, eyes closed. "What do you want?" Zane asked flatly, definitely less friendly now.

"He's running wild."

Zane gave her a look that said *no kidding*. Eve felt as if she were grasping at straws. "I have to find a way to contain him. Limit his opportunities for disaster."

"You're asking a lot."

She almost laughed. She couldn't believe Zane could make her crack a smile at a time like this. "I'm serious."

"So am I. Thomas is a kid inside an adult body."

"I've thought the same thing."

Zane stared down into his cup. "What do you want me to do?"

"Keep him here. Get him in the saddle. Work his butt off." She exhaled slowly, her breath ruffling her pale blond bangs. "I can't have him back in town until the film wraps. Ty's going to pay all the damages at the bar last night, but the owner doesn't want him, or my crew, anywhere near the place. I can control my crew, but Ty..." Her voice faded and she looked off into the distance. The horizon glowed brighter, yellow light radiating from behind the hills. "Ty's something else."

Zane sighed. "I'm going to need more coffee for this. Come on. I can tell you need a cup, too."

CHAPTER SEVEN

ZANE HADN'T EVEN POURED her coffee yet and he was already kicking himself for inviting her in.

This was how he got himself in trouble. He looked at her. He listened to her. He responded to her.

Damn, he was soft.

Maybe if he didn't have sisters, he wouldn't care so much about a woman's feelings. He'd love not to care. He'd love to turn his back, say Eve's problems weren't any of his concern and wish her luck. But somehow he couldn't. And that pissed him off more than anything.

She smiled her thanks as he handed her the mug of fresh, steaming coffee. He didn't smile back. He was still too mad at her. How could she have taken Thomas's side instead of his? Thomas was an idiot. An idiot who didn't deserve a beautiful, real woman like Eve.

Suddenly Zane knew why Adam got into trouble in the Garden of Eden. Eve was just too damn sexy.

His Eve was just too sexy, too. Even without a hint of makeup and her hair pulled back in a scruffy ponytail, she looked sinful. Remembering the way she'd felt in his arms when they danced made his groin ache and desire surge.

Damn, she confused the hell out of him.

Now she was looking at him with wide blue eyes,

all worry and regret. "I'm sorry about the other night. Ty was really insulting."

He didn't trust himself to speak.

"I was afraid you'd ruin his face," she added carefully, her gaze dropping to the heavy mug she held between her hands. "We're already behind schedule. I couldn't even imagine what would happen if we had to wait for a black eye to heal."

"He's your star. You have to protect him."

"It's not that. I just knew Ty wouldn't listen to me."

"And I would?"

She blushed. "You respect me." She fidgeted miserably. "But I'm sorry if I hurt you. I didn't want to hurt you."

She hadn't hurt him. She couldn't. But as his gut balled up tight, he knew he was lying through his teeth.

He was losing his head, losing perspective. She wasn't the answer to his loneliness. She wasn't a solution to the emptiness. She was a beautiful woman, but he couldn't start making plans for a future. There'd be no future with someone like Eve. She wasn't the type to stick around. She had a demanding career, and playing house with him outside Reno, Nevada, wasn't on her agenda.

What he needed to do was get her out of his hair and back to L.A. as soon as possible, but that wouldn't happen until the film wrapped, and the film couldn't wrap if they couldn't even get started.

"This isn't going to work," he said roughly, thinking he needed to get some control again. He needed distance between him and Eve, not closer proximity. "I understand you've got your hands full with pretty boy, but he's not my responsibility, and frankly, I couldn't work with him. He's too spoiled. Too lazy. I wouldn't put up with his crap.''

''Then don't. He'd be here on your property, working for you.''

Zane laughed without humor. ''He'd never do it.''

She shrugged. ''Then the movie doesn't get made.''

His eyebrows formed a flat line. She couldn't mean that. If she didn't pull this off, she'd never get any respect in the business. ''You'd be ruining your career.''

Her lips twisted in a painful smile. ''It'd be ruined, anyway, if we continue as we are, wasting hundreds of thousands of dollars each day we don't shoot. The bottom line is that Ty's drinking is ruining the production. The last director was fired because he read Ty the riot act—''

''And you're not afraid of the same fate?''

''Do I have a choice? His behavior is destroying morale on the set. Most of the crew can barely tolerate him, and the cast has lost respect for him. All I can do now is play hardball.''

Zane studied her pale face with the two bright spots of color burning in her cheeks. She looked so damn beautiful right now, so determined to succeed.

He had to admire her. He liked courage. Liked confidence, too.

But the more he was drawn to her, the more cautious he felt. ''I've got work to do, Eve. Baby-sitting Thomas would be a full-time job.''

''I'll supervise him. I'll sleep in the bunkhouse with him. I'll be on him twenty-four-seven. All you have to do is get him to ride.''

Zane shot her a swift glance. He'd heard via his

brother that Ty had spent yesterday at Patti's Stables. "How'd he do with Patti?"

"Not good."

Patti was a great woman, and a friend of his sister, but he knew Patti was more accustomed to working with sweet kids than petulant movie stars.

Zane thought about Ty and his attitude at the bar, and suddenly knew he'd give his eyeteeth for a chance to teach Ty a thing or two. Maybe it wouldn't be so bad having pretty boy here. He could give the guy some riding lessons, and while he was at it, a couple of lessons in humility, too.

Truthfully, there was no reason Ty couldn't sleep in the ranch bunkhouse. But Twin Bar Ranch wasn't the Hilton, and Zane's men wouldn't tolerate any airs, either. While Zane had no problem with Ty bunking down with his men, there was no way he'd let Eve sleep there. Cowboys and ranch hands had their own code of conduct, and no-women-in-the-bunkhouse was one of the long-standing rules.

"You'd have to stay up at the house," he said flatly. "My guys won't tolerate any female stuff in their quarters."

"Female stuff?" she repeated indignantly.

"Makeup. Hair spray. *Lotions.*" He made the word sound like something deadly. "There's been a no-girls, no-frills rule as long as Twin Bar's been around."

She snorted. "That's utterly ridiculous. And sexist!"

"Doesn't matter. These are the ranch rules. Thomas sleeps in the bunkhouse. You sleep here. If you're uncomfortable with me in the house, I'll bed down at Zach's."

He hadn't forgiven her for the scene at McCornick and Weston's, she thought, heat rushing to her cheeks. He'd help her, but he was all business. "Do you want to draw up a contract?"

"Yes. If I'm going to devote the better part of the next couple days to teaching your star how to ride, I want to be paid for my time, and be reimbursed for Ty's room and board, as well."

They were definitely all business now. "No problem. You'll be paid the same rate we were paying for Ty's suite at the hotel in town. And I just ask that you bill me for your hours."

"I'm more expensive than Patti."

Eve grimaced. "I sure hope so. Because I'm counting on you to be better, too."

He surprised her by chuckling, the deep sound rumbling from his chest, and it was as sexy a laugh as Eve had ever heard. "We start this morning, then. As soon as he's awake."

"That could be a while. Ty can sleep all day if he wants to."

"Don't worry. I won't let him."

The front door opened and heavy footsteps echoed in the hall.

Zane looked at Eve, one eyebrow rising. "Sounds like Sleeping Beauty's awake, after all."

Eve tensed. "He's going to have one nasty headache."

"That's all right. I've got aspirin. And I promise he'll be in the saddle by the end of the morning."

Ty's footsteps creaked down the hall as he staggered into the kitchen. "What time is it?"

"Six." Zane leaned against the counter, hands

braced next to him. "I'm just about to get breakfast started. Have a seat at the table."

Ty pulled out a chair and sat down, slumping backward as if boneless, while Zane began cracking a half-dozen eggs into a bowl.

The sound of the whisk against the metal bowl drew a groan of protest from Ty, who covered his ears in near agony. "That's too loud."

Zane gave the eggs another quick turn before placing a pan on the stove. "Scrambled okay with everyone?"

"Sure," Eve answered.

"Don't want any," Ty mumbled miserably, eyes red-rimmed. "But I'd kill for a Bloody Mary."

Zane poured the eggs into the hot pan. "Sorry, pal, I don't keep alcohol in the house."

That silenced Ty for a few minutes, and Eve stood back, watching Zane work. He looked pretty comfortable in his kitchen. It was obvious he'd been a bachelor for a while and had learned to fend for himself.

Ty broke the silence with another miserable groan as he shifted forward, leaning heavily on the old oak table. "What are we doing here, anyway? I need sleep. I need to go to bed. I want to go to the hotel now."

Eve clasped her cup between her hands and studied Ty. He looked bad. He must have consumed a liter of something nasty last night. "Zane's got a place for you to stretch out."

"I don't want to sleep here. I want my own bed, my own room—"

"You don't have your own room anymore," she interrupted. "I've checked you out of the hotel. You're going to stay here until the movie wraps."

Ty glanced from Eve to Zane and back again. "What?"

Eve moved to the table, pulled out a chair across from Ty and sat down. "You're going to stay here, on the ranch, until we're finished on location."

"Why?"

"Because you've worn out your welcome in town, Ty, and we're behind schedule on the film. I need you here, I need you sober, and I need you ready to work."

For a moment, Ty didn't say anything, his expression utterly bewildered. The only sound was Zane dishing up the eggs.

Finally Ty shook his head. "I can't stay here."

"You don't have a choice."

"Sure I do," he flung, temper rising. "Remember how you got this job? It was me. I pulled the strings, and if you jerk me around, gorgeous, I'll pull the strings again."

A few weeks ago Eve would have felt threatened, but she was past the point of intimidation. She had a job to do and she intended to do it. "I'm not playing games. I'm going to make this movie, and so are you."

"Take me back to the hotel."

"No."

Ty swore and shifted back in his chair, causing the legs to bang against the hardwood floor. "I'll call Tim."

Tim Walton, the senior producer, was the man with the money. "And tell him what?" she demanded. "That you got arrested last night after another drunken brawl resulting in forty thousand dollars' damage?"

"Jesus," Ty muttered, covering his face.

"You can say that again." Eve glared at him. She was tired. Grouchy. Fed up.

Ty rubbed his face, then dropped his hands. "How am I going to get to Patti's house?" he asked after a moment, watching Zane as he loaded fried bacon onto the oversize plates.

Eve prayed for patience. "You won't be going back to Patti's. Zane's going to work with you."

Zane set a steaming plate in front of Ty. "Eve told me Patti Johnson's got you riding. That's great. Now I'll just hone your skills. Make you look professional."

Ty's blue gaze narrowed. "Is that a joke?"

With a shrug, Zane served the last two plates. "Do I look like I'm kidding around?"

Eve pressed one knuckled fist against the table. "We've already covered this, Ty. You have to look comfortable in the saddle, and besides riding, you're going to need a few other skills. Zane's got real rodeo experience."

"What kind of skills?" Ty demanded, folding his hands on top of his head.

"Roping. Sticking in the saddle when the horse wants you off."

Ty's hands fell and he pushed his plate of eggs away. He'd turned pale. "Bronco riding?"

"No. Just good horsemanship. Couple of basic skills," Zane answered calmly.

"Can't do it."

"Sure you can. You're athletic. And smart. You'll master this stuff in a few days."

Ty looked positively green. "I can't do it," he repeated numbly. "In fact, I know I can't do it."

"Do what? Rope?"

"No." Ty swallowed hard. "The riding part. The part where the horse runs and bucks and tries to throw me off—"

"That's not going to happen," Zane interrupted, his tone firm, authoritative.

"Yeah?" Beads of perspiration covered Ty's brow. His breathing was quick, shallow, and his fingers clenched the edge of his green place mat. "You don't know me."

"Maybe not. But I know my horses."

"You can never know a horse." Ty was growing paler still. "They're temperamental."

"Some, not all."

Stumbling to his feet, Ty announced, "I'm going to be sick."

Zane stood, gestured with his thumb. "The john's down the hall. Second door to the left."

Eve looked at Zane as Ty raced out, his trembling hand all but covering his mouth. Perfectly calm, Zane sat down again, pulled his plate closer and stabbed a fork into his eggs. He took a bite, then another.

But Eve couldn't eat. She sat frozen, listening to the retching sounds down the hall. "He's terrified. I had no idea he was so deathly afraid of horses."

"He's throwing up because he had too much to drink last night and the smell of eggs pushed him over the edge." Zane looked across the table at her. "And yeah, he's afraid right now, but I think he'll settle down. He'll be all right."

She heard Ty retch yet again and felt her own stomach heave. "How can you be so sure?"

Zane shrugged. "I just know."

Footsteps sounded in the hall and Ty's shadow stretched across the kitchen floor.

"Hey," he said on his return, his expression more than a little sheepish. "Sorry about that."

"Not a problem." Zane said, leaving his chair to cross the kitchen floor. He opened a bag of sliced sandwich bread. "Eggs might be a bit much on an upset stomach. How about some toast?"

ZANE HAD TY IN THE SADDLE after breakfast. Even though Ty looked green, he was trying hard to focus. Within an hour they left the corral for a short trail ride, beads of perspiration gleaming on Ty's brow. With Zane in the lead, Ty followed more slowly behind, his knuckles nearly white as he gripped the reins.

Eve was still waiting when they returned forty some minutes later. Ty slid from the saddle as soon as he reached the corral and staggered away from the horse.

"It didn't go well, did it?" she said to Zane as he picked up the reins from Ty's horse.

"He did fine."

Eve shook her head. "He doesn't look fine." She watched as Ty stumbled from view, disappearing around the back of the barn. "I think he's going to get sick again."

Zane loped the leather reins around a corral post. "Wouldn't be surprised. He got sick on the trail."

"What!"

He shrugged. "I wouldn't get all worked up. Throwing up isn't the end of the world. He's a bit shaky now, but he'll pull through."

Eve wasn't so sure. This was agony. Ty was in agony. She couldn't do this to him. She didn't feel right doing this— She stopped herself.

Why was she feeling sorry for him? He'd chosen to stay out half the night drinking. They hadn't forced this role on him, either. He knew the story, had read the script and fought for the part despite being terrified of horses, and to top it off, he'd lied about his experience. Why should she feel pity for him? He was making five million dollars to boot.

"You know, I used to think I was really tough," she said. "But I'm not. I'm just like my dad. There's a reason he didn't make it in Hollywood—"

"Don't," Zane interrupted, touching her arm.

Her skin felt hot where he'd touched her. "I waited my whole life for this opportunity and I'm blowing it, Zane. I thought that once the script shaped up, we'd be okay. I was sure once we actually got here, on location, we'd start making progress, but we're not moving forward. We just keep moving back."

Zane made an impatient sound. "Don't you run scared, too."

"I don't know if I'm running scared or just being honest with myself."

"Too bad. It's too late for that. You signed on for this film so you need to deliver."

The sharpness of his voice caught her by surprise. But before she could speak, he continued. "Yeah, you've got some pressure on you. And yeah, you've got a lead with some problems, but weren't you the one who said every movie was hard? Every production had some issues? So deal with them."

Suddenly Eve felt stupid and emotional. She reached up and pushed a tendril of hair from her face since her ponytail wasn't doing its job this morning. "I'm sorry."

"Don't apologize. We're just talking."

"I know. But I hate to be—don't want to be—" She couldn't finish because she couldn't say the word.

Weak. She hated the word, hated everything it represented. "A pushover," she concluded lamely.

"You're the last person I'd describe as a pushover. I think you're just tired. You could use some sleep."

Eve looked up at him. His expression had gentled and she would have loved to move into his arms, have him hold her again the way he had on the dance floor. "You'll never admit it, but you do like me a little, don't you?"

His eyes narrowed, but not before she saw a hint of a smile in the green depths. "You're tolerable."

She grinned. "Man, you have a way with words."

"A poet, I've been told."

Her smile stretched and she found herself feeling really good again. She felt the same warm happiness she'd known the other night at McCornick and Weston's before Ty arrived and ruined everything.

Ty. Just his name brought her back to reality and the responsibility on her shoulders. "I appreciate your support, Zane."

He shrugged, his expression definitely less easy. "You're not a charity case. I'm getting paid good money."

"But you said you didn't need the money."

His smile was wry. "And I didn't think you ever listened."

She'd never admit it to anyone, but she liked it when he teased her. "Give me one example when I didn't listen to you."

He held up one finger. "When I told you no about using the ranch for your location." He held up two fingers. "When I told you I wasn't going to help train Ty—"

"Okay, okay," she interrupted before he could come up with a third example. "I get the picture."

"Speaking of Ty," Zane drawled, catching sight of the actor staggering into view. "I've got my work cut out for me."

Her desire to laugh faded. "He is a mess."

A muscle pulled in Zane's jaw, and he appeared to be considering his words with care. "I'm not going to get all soft on you, and I'm not a fan of Thomas's, but there's something else going on here. Just like we both know I'm not helping you because I need the money, your actor didn't take this role for the five million, either. Something else is eating at him. That's the part you've got to figure out. Soon as you do, you'll be able to help him, and you'll get your movie done."

He was right.

He was absolutely right.

Eve blinked, startled by the insight. She looked at Ty, who'd taken a seat on the front steps of the bunkhouse. His shoulders slumped and his arms hung limply between his knees. "Why didn't I see that?"

"I only just figured it out myself."

"I'm impressed."

He shrugged. "Even rednecks have brains."

Eve didn't mean to, but she laughed out loud. Zane had a way of hitting her funny bone. People always said she was too serious, that she didn't have much of a sense of humor, but when she was around Zane, she found herself almost constantly smiling. "Ty didn't hurt your feelings, did he?"

Zane snorted. "No way. But I have to say I am looking forward to teaching him how to ride—"

"Zane..."

"I just need forty-eight hours of his undivided attention and I'll have him ready to finish the movie."

"I don't want you to kill him."

"I won't."

Her eyebrows arched.

"I'll be patient," he said. "I'll be nice."

She made a small face. "Just like you were nice to him at the bar?"

"Hey, he picked the fight."

Silence stretched between them. She averted her head and let the sun play over her face, warming her. It was midmorning, but it felt like late afternoon to Eve. "Next time I'll take your side."

"Yeah, right." Zane pushed up his hat and looked at her hard. "Tell me something."

She turned to face him. "What?"

"Did you want to dance with Pretty Boy?"

"No," she answered softly, thinking that Zane might talk like a tough guy, all attitude and flinty emotion, but underneath he was so much more. "I didn't want to dance with Ty. I was dancing with you. I only wanted to dance with you.

He continued to hold her gaze, and silence stretched yet again, but this time the silence was charged with tension. Had she given him the right answer? Was this what he wanted to know?

But then he dispelled her uncertainty with a slow smile. "Good."

His smile was her undoing. She felt her stomach do a crazy flip. Then he reached up and dragged his hat lower on his head, the brim once again shielding his stormy green eyes. "Now, head on back to town, pack up your things and let me get to work. You've given me a job here, and I intend to see it done."

CHAPTER EIGHT

BACK AT THE HOTEL, Eve showered, dressed and, after ordering a pot of tea from room service, sat down at her desk to check her voice mail messages. There were twenty-three messages to be exact, which could only mean one thing: word had gotten out about Ty's arrest last night.

She didn't even bother to listen to all the messages. She knew the studio would be livid, and her job could be in jeopardy. She had to call the studio immediately.

"You've seen the papers?" Tim Walton demanded, the moment his assistant put Eve through. "Have you lost all control? What the hell is going on up there? You were supposed to be an improvement, not the kiss of death."

This was just Tim in his bulldog mode, she told herself. "We're making good progress."

"So Thomas wasn't arrested, and he didn't spend the night in jail?"

"No, that part is true."

"And the article in *Variety?* The claim that Thomas is afraid—no, make that *terrified*—of horses?"

Damn it. How had that gotten leaked to the press? Who had known, and who had talked? She hated being a fill-in director. The crew wasn't hers. She'd inherited them along with the script, problem actor and remote location, but Eve was determined to make this work.

Before addressing Tim's question, she made a mental note to find out who was leaking confidential information to the press. "Of course Ty can ride a horse." She glanced behind her, hearing the sound of a vacuum in the hallway. "Why couldn't he?"

"The article says—"

"It's rubbish." Her stomach was in knots, and her head felt like it was going to explode. "Ty's a natural. You should see him. I've got him on location with an ex-rodeo pro right now and he's doing great."

Eve tried not to picture Ty staggering around and throwing up in Zane's bushes.

"But you're still not filming?" Tim asked.

"We're filming." She plugged her ear to block the vacuum noise. "The crew's out right now, doing landscape shots—hills, clouds, shadows, sky, panoramas. Later this afternoon we're shooting the fight scene. The choreographer's rehearsing the actors now."

Tim made a rough sound in the back of his throat. "This is a damn expensive film, Caffrey. Ty alone costs a fortune."

"I'm fully aware of that."

The producer released a string of curses under his breath. He had a reputation for being on the abrasive side, but he was truly worked up now. "You know what an article like this in *Variety* can do?"

She did. Too well. Some reporter had once flippantly called her father a "B-movie hack" in *Variety,* and that phrase stuck. The cruel description had appeared in every article about her father since then. "We'll get some good PR."

"How?"

"Invite Peggy from *Inside Hollywood* to visit. Peggy loves going on location."

"Not a bad idea. I've heard she's a sucker for cow-boys. I'll have our publicist get on it. See if we can't get a film crew up today or tomorrow."

"I was thinking more like next week."

"Next week's too late. Tell me, is this ex-rodeo rider any good? What's his commercial appeal?"

Tall, muscular and sexy.

But she didn't say any of that. There was no way she'd make a story out of Zane. "He knows his horses," she answered flatly. The noise in the hall abruptly stopped. "But he wouldn't be good on film. He's pretty…private."

"What's his name? We'll look him up with the PRCA," he said, referring to the Professional Rodeo Cowboy Association. "See if we can't dig up a feel-good story."

Eve's heart fell. She couldn't let this happen. Zane would hate the attention. He hated fuss of any kind. She couldn't even imagine how he'd react to a tele-vision tabloid show tramping all over his property and sticking microphones and cameras in his face.

The vacuum started up again. Her nerves screamed, on edge. Zane could not be the focus of a publicity push. She would not let that happen. Instead she had to come up with another angle, something that would give Ty some positive press, which he desperately needed.

"I've another idea," she said, battling to keep the tension from her voice. She couldn't get into a power play with Tim. She'd lose, big time. "It'd take a few days to put together, but if you send out a fun invite— get your publicists to get creative—we could start a positive buzz now."

"What's your idea?"

Eve closed her eyes, pressed her fingers against her brow. Her brain raced as she tried to think of a way to turn this around without it blowing up in her face. How to generate some warm fuzzies at the last minute?

She knew the media would go nuts if they saw Twin Bar Ranch and the old stone calvary outbuildings. They'd love Ty in tight jeans and cowboy boots. She'd need him on a horse, and that made her nervous, but it was time Ty started to carry his own weight.

Then it came to her. "A press conference." She pictured a western-theme picnic out on the lawn between Zane's house and the rustic stone stable. Ty could ride around on his horse and look gorgeous, and then make some small talk with the media. "We could probably pull something western together without too much effort. Everybody around here loves barbecues. Give them some chicken and corn on the cob and it might work."

"If Ty can ride a horse."

"He can ride a horse." She swallowed hard. *Almost.*

"All right, then, I like it. We'll handle the press invites from here. I'll have the girls in Media Relations get on it right away. I'm going to put some money into this. We need to dazzle. We need to look good."

Eve didn't know about dazzle, but the ranch itself was beautiful and Zane was pretty amazing. The question was whether or not Ty could pull the big-star personality off, and how Zane would react to having a bunch of reporters herded all over the ranch.

Maybe she needed to get rid of him for a few days. Send him to Lake Tahoe, or even to his brother Zach's. "How fast could we make it happen?"

Tim had been in the business more than fifteen years. "Couple days. Three or four."

"You think we could get a decent turnout on such short notice?"

"I've never known the press to turn down a free trip anywhere. We'll charter some planes. Get some buses to meet them at the airport. We can start the fun here, and then continue once the media arrives at the ranch."

"It's Thursday today," he said, thinking out loud. "We could schedule for Sunday, which would give us almost three days to put it together, and you won't waste another day not filming."

Three days to get Ty ready. Three days to make him look like a pro. "Sounds great."

"The publicity department will be in touch as soon as we start getting details firmed up."

She didn't remember what she said, but once she hung up, her confidence failed her.

Eve sat at the desk and stared blankly at the wall as her brain did a slow fry. She'd just suggested throwing a press party on a ranch that wasn't her property, with an actor who couldn't ride, and it all was going to happen three days from now. She was either really stupid, or really brave, and no matter which, she needed her head examined.

She'd call a meeting with her cast and crew this afternoon to break the news. No one—including her assistant director—was going to like giving up their Sunday, especially not to spend the day with the press. But business was business, and Hollywood was all business.

After checking out of the hotel, Eve drove back to Twin Bar Ranch with her suitcase, her computer and boxes of production notes filling the trunk of her rental car.

Her instinct had been right. As soon as she told the cast and crew about the press conference, they bitterly complained at giving up their one day off. They were already working the standard six-day week. Going seven was a hardship.

"Sorry, folks," Eve said as kindly as she could, "but we have to do what we have to do."

Someone mumbled that Ty Thomas was screwing it up for everyone else, and someone else retorted that maybe it was time the Aussie did what he had to do, since he was the one getting paid the big money.

Eve looked out at the unhappy crew clustered before her. The already rocky relations on the set were just getting worse. "I know it's frustrating—"

"'Frustrating' doesn't even begin to cover it," one of the makeup artists muttered.

"But that's the way it is," Eve said flatly, her voice sounding hard. "Life happens. We deal with it."

"Yeah, we're dealing with it all right," a member of the lighting crew groused. "I hate working for female bosses. They always get their panties bunched up their—"

"Knock it off." It was Ty. He'd been standing at the edge of the tent where Eve had convened the meeting. "You got a problem, blame me, mates. But leave Eve alone."

With those words, the general meeting ended, and most of the cast and crew dispersed. Ty approached Eve as she gathered the notes needed for a briefing with her production staff. They had to map out the scenes being shot this afternoon to minimize time loss.

Eve glanced up at Ty. "I don't need you sticking up for me. I can handle them."

"I just don't think it's fair—"

"No, what's not fair is that you're not doing the job you were hired to do. You're not pulling your weight, Ty. This is your film. You're the star and you're screwing up big time."

He stared at her for a long moment, his blue eyes hard, and then his expression eased. "I'm not trying to screw things up."

"Then what the hell is going on? This isn't like you! You've always had a strong work ethic—"

"It's personal," he interrupted tersely.

"Obviously." She didn't have time for this. Didn't have time for lies or excuses. Ty's career wasn't the only one on the line. Lots of people depended on this film and were going to be hurt if it didn't succeed. "Make this work. I don't know what you have to do, Ty, but make this film work."

They spent the afternoon filming and managed to put a short but pivotal scene in the can. The moment they wrapped the scene, Zane appeared.

"We've got work to do," he said, gesturing to Ty. "Eve, you need him anymore today or can I have him?"

Eve shot Ty a hard glance, her patience shot. "He's all yours."

The next few days passed quickly, with intensive sessions on the set. Eve and her production team went through the script and attempted to move up the filming of scenes that didn't require riding skills or stunt-work. But each schedule change meant set changes, costume and prop changes, even choreography changes, which were all costly in terms of time and money. The crew was definitely getting testy, but there was no way she could give them the day off they needed.

Although Eve slept at Zane's house, she saw even less of him than before. When she retired at night he was out, and by the time she woke the next morning, he was already gone. During the day he tackled his ranch jobs early, and hunted down Ty once his work was out of the way.

It wasn't until Saturday noon when a big truck from Reno rolled to a stop in Zane's drive that Eve realized she hadn't spoken to him yet about the media conference scheduled for tomorrow.

She had to get his approval fast, but when she went to look for him, she discovered that Zane and Ty had gone out for an afternoon ride. Ty wasn't in the scenes they were filming that afternoon, so Zane must have decided to take advantage of his free time.

Fighting nerves, Eve watched as the party-rental company rigged up more big white tents and began setting up tables and chairs. Native American blankets were draped over the tables, and lassos and saddles were strategically placed at the entrance of the tents. Eve didn't even want to imagine what Zane's reaction would be if she didn't get to him first.

IT WAS ALMOST FOUR-THIRTY when Zane neared the house. He and Ty had a quarter of a mile to go, and Zane couldn't wait to get back and get a long, cold drink and pop a couple of aspirin for his shoulder.

He stretched now, then felt along the deltoid muscle, checking for tears. Probably the rotator cuff. It would heal. Thank goodness that was the worst of the damage, considering the crazy stunt he'd pulled trying to calm Ty's panicked horse when Ty stumbled across a rattler sunning on a flat rock.

Sighing, Zane glanced over his shoulder at the Australian actor. He didn't blame Ty for panicking, though. Ty's horse had reared back, instinctively reacting to the rattle, and that same instinct had driven the mare to try to smash the coiled snake rather than running away.

But Ty lost it. He couldn't get off the horse fast enough, and then the poor confused mare tried to bolt. Zane literally threw himself from one saddle into another to keep the high-strung Arabian from disappearing.

Looking back at Ty, Zane almost felt sorry for him. Thomas was still pale and shaky. The actor hadn't wanted to get back into the saddle, but Zane insisted. It had been a ten-minute battle of wills, but in the end, Zane won, and a very tight-lipped Ty climbed onto the skittish horse's back.

Zane's gaze met Ty's now, and Ty urged his horse to pick up the pace until he rode alongside Zane. "Sorry about that, mate," he said huskily.

Zane nodded, the brim of his hat shielding his eyes.

Ty reached up and adjusted his own hat. Zane had made sure Ty was wearing appropriate trail clothes when they left the stable. The heels on the boots allowed him to plant his feet in the stirrups, and the Stetson provided protection from sun and rain. The boots had paid off doubly this afternoon when the rattler went for Ty's ankles.

"You're sure she's going to be all right?" Ty persisted, reaching down to pat the mare's neck. "I'd hate to have hurt her."

He'd been really shaken, Zane thought, studying

Ty's grim-set features. The rattler, the runaway horse, the crazy adrenaline had done something to Ty. He looked positively shell-shocked, and Zane knew something else was going on here, something that had nothing to do with the snake or being thrown by his horse.

"She's fine," Zane answered, shooting Ty another close look from beneath the brim of his hat. "How 'bout you?"

"I'm okay. Thanks."

But he wasn't okay. Zane knew without a doubt now that Ty was battling something bigger than fear of horses. Something horrific had happened in his past....

Zane resolved to talk to Eve about Ty's fear as soon as they returned. The young actor might need more help than what Zane could give him.

When they rode around the back of the barn, they practically slammed into a big white truck with Reno's Number #1 Party Source painted on the side.

"What the hell?" Zane swore.

"They're setting up for the media event," Ty told him, leaning forward in his saddle and getting a look at the two-dozen-odd vehicles choking the drive.

"What media event?"

Ty sat up a little straighter and gathered the reins loosely in one hand. "Looks as if somebody forgot to tell our host." He set off toward the white tent on the lawn near the house.

Seething, Zane followed but rode more slowly. He felt tricked. Betrayed. Eve had said she wanted a quiet place for Ty to work. She wanted him to nail his skills in relative seclusion. So what the hell was going on here?

As he neared the tent, he spotted Eve standing on

the side of a wood platform. Ty was there already, talking to her and some of the crew.

Eve felt a wave of tension and a ripple of awareness. She turned around and slowly surveyed the outbuildings before spotting Zane. He was still on his horse and he looked really angry.

Her stomach knotted. He wasn't going to be an easy sell, she thought, stepping off the platform and walking toward him. "Hi."

He wouldn't make eye contact. "What's going on?"

"It's all for a mini press conference we're throwing together."

"When?"

"Tomorrow."

"Why?"

She'd known deep down he wouldn't like all these folks here. She'd known he'd be upset, but she'd ignored her reservations and pushed on because this film was everything to her. "We need the publicity—to create a positive buzz after Ty's latest fiasco."

"And the press is coming here?"

"Yes," she answered quietly, even as she wondered if her job demanded too much of her, forcing her to take advantage of others too often.

"You should have asked me first. This is my home. I *live* here."

"I know. And I'm sorry."

He gave a brief, frustrated shake of his head and slid off his horse. "This is a big mistake."

There was such disgust in his voice that Eve's eyes burned and a lump formed in her throat. She took a step toward him. "You were the one who told me it was too late for second thoughts, and too late to quit.

You told me just a few days ago that it was my job to deliver, and that's what I'm trying to do. So don't you make me feel bad for fighting for this film. It's been a nightmare, but I'm trying to see my way clear.''

He stared at the white tent for a moment without speaking, his gaze focused on Ty. ''Something is going on with him. Something bigger than your average fear of horses, and I don't think it's wise doing a big press conference until you know what it is.''

''I'm not a shrink, Zane.''

''You don't have to be a shrink to see that he's genuinely chewed up about something. The thing is, and here's what I should have told you a couple days ago—'' Zane broke off and pushed his hat back. ''Ty can ride.''

''What?''

''He can rope, too. Thomas isn't the city boy he wants you to think he is.'' Zane met Eve's startled gaze and his lips curved. ''Zach's looking into something for me, but I'd be willing to bet that your movie star's first pair of shoes were boots. I imagine he grew up sitting in the back of an old flatbed pickup. And ten to one, he's a redneck just like me.''

Eve was speechless. One of Zane's eyebrows arched. ''You don't believe me?''

''Impossible,'' she said at last. ''Ty's from Sydney. He attended the prestigious arts program in the city—many of Hollywood's big Australian stars graduated from the NIDA—''

''Or so he says.'' Zane reached up and rubbed his shoulder. ''Anyway, for your information, Ty took a tumble earlier. His horse stumbled across a rattlesnake, bucked, and Ty panicked. He ended up getting thrown.

I don't think he broke anything, but you might want
to have him checked by a doctor, just in case.''

Eve noticed Zane's ripped shirt for the first time,
and then the bloodstains on the sleeve. ''And did you
get attacked by the snake, too?''

''Snake's not that fast. I just had to stop Ty's horse.
Got spooked by all the activity.''

''I bet.''

His green eyes, which moments ago had been
smoky with anger, softened and warmed. ''You really
do owe me, Miss Caffrey.''

''I know.''

THE CATERING TRUCKS ARRIVED the next morning and
so did the floral deliveries. Catering was using real
cast-iron skillets and woven baskets for the menu, and
old-fashioned lanterns to provide light.

The first of the silver passenger buses drove over
the cattle guard at noon. By one o'clock there were
more than a dozen cars and buses lining the driveway.

The presentation was scheduled to start at one-
thirty. Smoothing her honey-colored blazer over her
crisp white blouse, Eve headed for the platform. At
the podium she saw the throng of reporters and cameramen jostling for closer access to the bar. Tim had
been right. Few people could resist freebies.

The press had noticed Eve at the podium and conversation died as they moved toward the folding
chairs. On the seat of each chair was a colorful press
kit featuring production notes, actor biographies and a
history of Nevada. The prized goodie bags beneath
each seat were stuffed with a rustic silver watch em-
bedded with bits of turquoise, a volume of cowboy
poetry, twin bottles of fragrance, his and hers, a classic

red bandanna and massive chewy molasses cookies with the recipe attached.

Turning on the microphone, Eve talked about the bestselling novel, *American Jack*, and how it was developed into a screenplay. She described casting and scouting for the perfect location, mentioning that there would be a tour of the ranch's historic calvary buildings later in the afternoon. Then began the cast introductions. A number of the crew had been asked to talk, and they did, followed by a few cast members, and finally Ty.

But when Eve called Ty's name, he didn't step forward to the podium. She waited a moment before announcing his name again. "He's here somewhere," she joked, turning and craning her head to see if he'd stepped off to the side. "I saw him with a handful of those amazing molasses cookies just a few minutes ago."

"Maybe he headed back to that saloon in Reno!" a reporter shouted from the crowd. Everyone laughed.

"Maybe," she answered, hands pressed to the sides of the podium. "Or maybe he's out fighting rattlesnakes."

She caught their attention with that one. "It's true," Eve said. "It happened yesterday. You'll have to ask Ty for the details, but it was a big snake and the rattler had fangs four inches long."

"Not four, Eve, two."

The crowd gasped and laughed as Ty rode into the tent on his horse. He'd been miked, and wardrobe had dressed him in authentic western gear—boots, chaps, shirt, hat. As he reined in his horse by the platform, he leaned on the saddle's pommel. "She's right about one thing, though, it was a big snake. The important thing is that we didn't hurt him, and he didn't hurt us. It was a happy Hollywood ending for everyone.''

Eve stepped back and let Ty take over. The crowd, she noticed, loved him. They might be jaded entertainment reporters, but Ty had more charm in his little pinkie than most people had in their whole body. As Ty talked, the journalists scribbled notes and tape ran in video cameras.

As Eve stood on the side, listening to Ty spin stories the way only he could, Zane joined her. ''How's he doing?'' Zane asked softly.

''Great. This is the Ty I've worked with in the past. This is the Ty that I believe in.''

''His real name is Tommy Williams. His father is Buck Williams and one of the toughest SOB's Zach's ever met—''

''How do you know that? It's not part of his bio.''

'''Course not. There's nothing of his real past in his bio. The Ty Thomas the public sees is a new invention. It's a character he created.''

Eve's throat was dry and her mouth tasted like cotton. ''Zach knows Ty's dad?''

''They met at a big livestock auction a couple years ago. Buck talked a lot. He drank a lot, too. More than he should have.'' Zane glanced at Ty, who still held the crowd in his spell. ''Buck manages one of the biggest cattle spreads in the Territory—''

''Territory?'' she interrupted, her head spinning.

''Northern Territory. Huge part of Australia, but very remote. You have to be pretty self-sufficient to survive out there. It's a place you don't drive to. You fly in.''

''And you're telling me Ty was raised there?''

"Yeah. In the Outback. Ty and his brothers were practically born in the saddle."

She couldn't believe it. Ty Thomas, son of a ranch foreman? Ty Thomas, an Australian cowboy? It just didn't make sense. "So what's with Ty not being able to ride?" she whispered. "Is it just a big act? An attempt to get attention?"

"I don't think so. Zach said Buck had talked about something happening to a couple of his sons. I don't know the details, but I'm pretty sure your movie star witnessed something horrible and he's done everything in his power to distance himself from the past."

"Why would he take this part, then? *American Jack* is a turn-of-the-century cowboy."

Zane shrugged. "That I can't tell you. Maybe you need to ask him."

The air was suddenly pierced with a sharp whistle. Eve and Zane looked up and saw Ty waving at them.

"And there he is," Ty said, gesturing Zane forward. "Zane Dumas, one of the finest riders you'd ever hope to meet, and I'm going to ask him if he won't show you a thing or two in the corral behind us."

Zane shot Eve a sharp glance. "Did he just say what I thought he said?"

The crowd didn't waste any time. They were leaving their seats and heading en masse to the corral. "I think so," she said, uncertain if she should laugh or cry. "They're certainly excited."

Zane swore and pushed up the brim of his hat. His green eyes locked with hers and held. "You owed me before, but you *really* owe me now, Movie Girl."

CHAPTER NINE

EVE GLANCED AT THE REPORTERS and cameramen jockeying for position at the edge of the corral. "What do you want?"

Zane took a step away, giving her a view of the sexiest backside she'd ever seen.

He turned and caught her staring. When she blushed, his gaze scanned her face, moving leisurely from her eyes to her flushed cheeks and then to her mouth. "What can you offer me?" he retorted.

She felt herself grow hotter. "My undying gratitude?"

He snorted. "Already have that."

God, she loved it when he looked at her like that. As if she were something edible and delicious and meant to be savored on the tongue. "Money?"

"You're already paying me salary, location expenses, plus room and board, so I have enough of that already, thank you."

His eyes were teasing her, daring her, curious to see how far she'd go. Eve dragged in a breath. "A credit in the film?"

"Hardly find that interesting."

She could hardly breathe. The air felt hot and still. "You have any ideas?"

"Yeah." His eyes were melting her insides, turning her into sweet butter. "I want a ride."

"A ride?"

"A ride, as in riding," he added, his tone huskier, distinctly playful. His voice was teasing and yet his eyes were intense, focused. "Do you ride?"

"Horses?" Heat radiated out to her arms and legs. Suddenly she was desperate to get her blazer off, unbutton her blouse and expose her overheated skin to some cool air.

Creases fanned from the corners of his eyes. "You ride something else?" he drawled ever so slowly.

Her face felt hot, her lips tender. She'd loved dancing with him, loved the casual chitchat, too, but this was something else altogether. This was primal. This was all fire and need, and she knew now that he'd be amazing in bed.

He knew all about making love.

Her mouth was dry and her heart hammered. She could even hear the blood drum in her ears. There were things she wanted to do with him, things she wanted to do *to* him, but first she had to get rid of Tim and the two dozen cameras.

Zane's heated gaze stroked her face, did crazy, wanton things to her insides all over again. "Your paparazzi are getting restless. Do we have a deal or not?"

They had a deal. Eve joined the throng at the corral, leaning against one rail, watching Zane lead a young Arabian stallion into the center of the ring. From what Ty had told her, Zane had hoped to get a saddle on the stallion yesterday, but the stallion had other ideas.

Ty broke through the crowd and came to stand beside Eve. "He's going to get his butt kicked," he muttered to Eve, keeping his voice down so the others wouldn't hear. "One of the ranch hands said this handsome rascal threw the boss five times earlier this week. Ranch record.''

Knowing that the black stallion had set a ranch record for bad behavior, Eve couldn't believe how patient Zane was with the horse today. Even though the young stallion kicked and tossed his head, balking at each of Zane's requests, Zane remained quiet, firm and gentle. He kept his voice calm and his touch soothing. Zane didn't need to use force. And he didn't resort to intimidation.

While the crowd was following Zane's progress with the stallion, Zach arrived, weaving his way through the reporters and camera crew to join Eve and Ty at the edge of the corral. "What's going on?" Zach asked, pointing at the cameras fixed on his brother.

"They're filming Zane," Eve whispered.

Zach's stunned expression said it all. "And he's *letting* them?"

"Pretty nice of him, isn't it?"

Zach grinned, his eyebrows arching. "Well, well, there's hope for him yet."

Eve held her breath as Zane, reins in hand, placed one foot in the stirrup and carefully eased himself into the saddle. The stallion stiffened, bent his knees and bucked. Zane hung on. Again the stallion bucked, kicking up his back legs, but Zane stayed in the saddle.

Zach tipped his hat back. "Dang, if that cowboy don't know how to ride."

Eve couldn't look away. "He's good, isn't he?"

"One of the best," Zach agreed. But no sooner had the words left his mouth than the horse reared back, forelegs pawing at the air. The stallion came down hard, then kicked high with his back legs, sending Zane flying.

The Arabian immediately calmed and walked to the far side of the corral, where he turned and gave Zane a look of pure contempt. For a moment there was stunned silence from the crowd pressing against the outside of the corral, and then Zach began to laugh.

The cameras still rolling, Zane glanced up, caught Eve's stunned expression and his brother's laughter. Then his lips tugged into a reluctant smile, and pushing himself to his feet, he brushed off the soft buff-colored chaps protecting his legs. "Round number two coming right up."

Zane was thrown two more times before the stallion finally gave up and tolerated rider and saddle. Then, and only then, did Zane hand the reins over to a stable hand. "Give him a good brush down and extra oats," he said.

As the stallion was led from the corral, the reporters erupted, shouting questions at Zane. Zane sauntered toward the fence, the leather chaps fastened around his lean hips flapping with every step. He ignored the crowd, ignored even his brother, and reached out for Eve's hand. "Come on. You owe me a ride."

Eve felt Zach's amused gaze. "Now? With everyone still here?"

"No reason to feel shy. You don't have to be inhibited with me."

Her cheeks burned. She knew exactly what he was talking about. "I'm not shy. We just happen to have a lot of people still hanging about."

"Ah, you want to do this in private."

"*Zane.*"

"Okay. I can wait. Let your reporters have their little ranch tour. But once they're gone, you're mine."

She rather liked the idea of being all his, and yet

even as Eve kept up polite conversation with some of the reporters, she found herself thinking about Zane and his remarkable performance in the ring. Why would he give up competing on the rodeo circuit if he was so good? And if he had so many strengths—intelligence, good looks, loving family, successful career—why was he still a bachelor?

She had to find out. She had to know. Eve had always loved mysteries, but the one surrounding Zane and his secret was especially important. How could there ever be a future if she didn't understand the past?

Two hours later, the last of the big silver buses left the Twin Bar, and the visiting studio heads took Ty out to dinner with them. Eve had refused the offer, citing work, but truthfully, she wanted time alone with Zane.

She tracked Zane down where he was working in the stable.

"All gone?" he asked, looking up from the saddle he was rubbing with saddle wax. Fine dust had settled in the creases at his eyes, and her fingers itched to reach up and wipe the dust from his cheekbones. Even dusty and dirty, Zane was incredibly male.

And sexy.

"Every last one of them," she answered, straddling a workbench. "I'm so glad that's over." All she wanted was to be alone with Zane, have an hour or so of his undivided attention.

The stable doors were open and the late afternoon sun bronzed Zane's skin. The muscles in his biceps bunched like knots of thick rope as he worked the wax into the saddle. Eve loved watching him work. She loved the way his T-shirt clung to his chest, outlining the broad plane of muscle and the hard, flat stomach below.

She grinned and looked away, trying desperately to get some control. She'd never had such a one-track mind before. "I think it went pretty well," she said, trying to hide her intense physical craving. She'd give just about anything for a kiss from him right now. A kiss…a touch…a night in his arms.

He looked up. "The cookies seemed to be a big hit. Everyone was munching on them."

"Worried about crumbs, Dumas?"

"No, Caffrey. I was just hoping there might be a few left over for me."

When she laughed, he smiled at her, and Eve's stomach did a little flip. If he kept smiling at her like that, she'd end up doing something stupid like throw herself against him, wrap her arms around his neck and kiss him until the clothes came off and his strong arms were around her.

"I've got twenty-five or so left over," she said breathlessly. "I'll send some to the bunkhouse and the rest to your kitchen."

"Great." He threw down his polishing rag. "How about that ride?"

Zane washed his hands and led a pretty chestnut mare from a stall in the stable. He quickly bridled and saddled her. "Now, let's get you in the saddle," he said, "or we could be here all night."

Eve stepped into his laced hands and reached for his shoulder to steady herself as he boosted her up with ease. Sitting down gingerly in the saddle, she shifted her weight, trying to get comfortable.

"How does that feel?" he asked, standing back and observing her.

"Hard," she said, referring to the shape of the saddle near the pommel.

An eyebrow lifted. "You don't like hard?"

"Depends where hard is."

He stepped forward and placed a hand on her thigh. "What about the stirrups?"

She jumped at the touch of his hand on her leg. "They feel like stirrups."

"How about the tension on your knees?" he asked, sliding his palm down her thigh to cup her kneecap. "The stirrup should support the leg, without hyper-extending."

His hand was so warm on her knee. "It feels fine."

"Good." He ran his fingers down her calf to circle her ankle. "In case you've forgotten, you control the horse with your legs, mainly your knees."

His hand covered her kneecap again, and she felt a shiver race through her. She loved the way he was touching her. He was really turning her on, making her want more of everything, including his hands on her hips, between her thighs....

He glanced up at her. "If you want Sunny to go faster, press with your heels here," he said, reaching for her heel and pressing it against the mare's ribs. "If we're riding uphill, or you're not sure of your balance, use your knees, but in general, your thigh muscles do the big work." His hand slid from her knee along the inside of her leg, all the way up to the apex of her thighs. She felt his knuckles brush the zipper of her slacks, and the heat of his hand burned through.

Eve sucked in a breath, her belly hot and tight, her senses swimming. She didn't think she'd be able to keep her seat much longer. She didn't want to be in the saddle. She wanted to be on Zane's lap.

His gaze settled on her mouth, and heat flared in his eyes. She wasn't the only one craving more contact.

"Do we really have to do this?" she croaked, her mouth dry. "What about a rain check?"

His lips curved, but he wasn't exactly smiling. "I think you're safer on the horse."

"Maybe I don't want safe." Her voice was but a whisper. She swung her leg over the pommel and slid down, landing on the ground with a soft thud.

"*Eve.*"

"What?"

"We're playing with matches here."

She lifted her chin a notch. "We're not kids."

"Which is why we should know better. At least I should know better. I'm not going to be good for you."

She felt the horse shift, bumping into her. "You don't know me, Zane. You don't know what I need."

"Well, I know what you don't need. You don't need more trouble, not when you've got a movie barely hanging together, producers threatening to fire you, a problem actor a heartbeat away from a nervous breakdown—" He broke off, clamped his jaw tight and shook his head. "You don't want me, Eve. I'll only complicate things."

"I'm thirty-five. Maybe I like complications."

He looked up, lashes slowly lifting until his sage-green gaze locked with hers. In his eyes she saw fire. Hunger. A hunger that would have scared her if she were younger. "You're a beautiful woman. You could have your pick of men—"

"I don't want my pick of men. I want you. I want a chance to get to know you."

"A chance for what?" he demanded, his husky

voice growing impatient, almost sharp. "I'm a dead-end street, darlin'. I've been down the relationship road once and won't do it again. I don't want to date. Marry. Fall in love. Have kids. None of it. It's not going to happen with me. Ever."

"Why?" she demanded, knowing he was referring to his past, and the secret tragedy he never shared.

"Because. It's just the way it is. There are some things you can't change, Eve, and this is one of them."

His tone was hard, and yet the intensity in his eyes held her transfixed. She couldn't look away even if she wanted to. "But you do want me," she whispered. "I know you're attracted to me."

Grooves formed on either side of his mouth and the silence stretched long.

"I'm going to give you a chance to walk out of this stable," he said after an endless pause. "I'd do it, Eve. I'd do it now, if I were you." His voice had dropped so low, as smooth as fine whiskey.

His fierce expression made her tremble inwardly, yet she held her ground. "And if I don't?"

The shake of his head was barely perceptible. "I'm not responsible for what might happen next."

A shiver raced down her spine, cold, wild, fleeting. She loved this. She shouldn't, but she did. He was fire and ice and smoke and heat and she couldn't resist. "What might happen?"

He reached out, his long arms beautifully shaped with muscle, and caught her by the waist. Drawing her forward, against him, he slowly slid his hands down her waist, over her hips, until his thumbs grazed her hipbones.

It was an incredibly erotic touch, and Eve gasped,

lips parting. Zane's eyes focused on her mouth, and her soft sigh of pleasure.

Slowly he stroked her hipbones again. It was the craziest, most intense sensation, yet they were barely touching. He was just holding her by the hips, caressing the curve of her bone, but it felt as if her nerve endings were exploding.

As he strummed her again, her eyes drifted closed and she swayed a little on her feet, growing light-headed. Explosive.

Like that very first day she met him, when she'd been aware of the intense chemistry between them.

This, she thought, as he propelled her back, had been inevitable from the beginning. This attraction was like a gravitational force. Impossible to ignore. Impossible to resist.

She felt her shoulders make contact with Sunny's warm side and the stirrup bumping against her thigh. Her body shook as Zane ran his palm down the outside of her taut thigh, and then up again, until his fingers were against her zipper.

"Open your legs," he said, his mouth against her ear. "Open your legs for me."

She'd done sexy before, she'd done provocative, too, but nothing had prepared her for this. Her knees nearly buckled as she widened her stance.

Zane pushed her feet even farther apart and she felt his hand on her hip and his boot at her ankle. She shuddered as his fingers trailed down her thigh, making her aware of herself, her desire, her fierce need to be touched by him.

His eyes held hers, and color darkened his strong cheekbones. Still holding her firmly, he stepped between her thighs, the hard ridge in his jeans snug against her body. There was no escape from the sensation, or the pleasure. The stirrup dug into the back of her legs, his silver belt buckle pressed against her middle, and the hard length of him throbbed between her thighs.

The thin fabric of her wool slacks was no match for him. Even contained by the rough denim of his jeans, he was hard and hungry for her.

His eyes never leaving hers, he lifted her right arm over her head, and then her left, his hands pressing her back against the smooth leather saddle. She was trapped and exposed, and even that felt incredibly exciting. Her imagination hadn't misled her. He was definitely all man, and she found his strength and size thrilling.

"What's going to happen?" he repeated, voice deep, rough with passion. "I think you know."

The heat in his eyes seared her. The desire, no longer hidden, was there for her to see, and she'd never seen a hunger so raw before. It shocked her a little. It excited her even more.

Her heart was beating wildly. She could feel its ragged rhythm, and it matched the coiling in her belly. He leaned against her, his hips brushing hers, his chest grazing her sensitized breasts, her nipples already hard, tight, needing attention.

She was dying for him to touch her, really touch her. She wanted to feel his hands on her bare skin, feel his mouth on her lips, feel the hard pressure of his body against her.

His gaze dropped, and he looked down at her, savoring the full thrust of her breasts, the length of her taut abdomen, the curve of her hips. Then his eyes met hers again. "Don't say you haven't been warned."

When he released her, she would have fallen if she hadn't clutched the saddle with one hand. She was so dizzy she could barely see straight.

"No kiss?" she asked, flushing at her audacity and yet knowing that this was one man she wanted to know every way possible.

He gave his head a slight, bemused shake. "I'm on the sweaty side, don't you think?"

Eve swallowed hard, trying to calm the crazy staccato of her pulse. "I'm not afraid of sweat," she said, lifting her head and meeting his gaze. "I'm not afraid of sex. And I'm not afraid of you."

He stared at her for what felt like an eternity. "I don't want you afraid of me. I just want you to be sure you know what you're doing. I'm not a playboy. Or an actor. And this isn't a movie set. I'm not an easy person to get to know, but my feelings do run deep."

Feelings. He'd just admitted he had feelings. She lifted her chin. "I like you, Zane," she said quietly. "I want to be with you. More than I've wanted to be with anyone—ever."

"I'm going to head back and take a shower, and then I'll put some coals on the barbecue and grill some steaks. This is what I want—dinner, your company, a chance to unwind. After that, we'll talk, and then we'll decide whether or not we're going to make love."

He made it sound awfully grim, and yet when Zane returned from his bedroom, hair wet, freshly shaven, wearing clean jeans and a soft denim shirt, Eve knew for the first time what it was like to crave a man.

He shot her a curious look as he ignited the coals,

but other than that one quick glance, everything seemed very normal, almost too relaxed. Zane's shoulders were loose, his movements easy. He had that look that athletes get after a long run.

Eve was sure Zane had stamina.

It was odd, she'd never been so preoccupied with bodies before. But then she'd never met anyone with such a strong physical presence as Zane.

"Can I pour you a glass of wine?" he asked, leaving the barbecue on the side yard and climbing the steps to the house.

He passed so close to her she could feel his heat, his energy tangible. "You don't drink."

"I don't drink, but you can."

He'd stopped in the doorway and was looking at her. Her eyes locked with his, and suddenly she forgot what they were talking about, forgot everything but the way her heart pounded double time and her pulse raced.

There it was again. He was turning her inside out. Making her want things she'd never wanted before…an Ozzie-and-Harriet life. A life with stability, security, love and marriage and kids.

Eve blinked as Honey Bear padded up, long blond tail wagging. Make that marriage and kids and dog and a split-rail fence, Eve corrected.

Zane leaned down to scratch behind Honey's ears. "I'm not uncomfortable with others drinking, and I told Ty we didn't have liquor because I didn't want him looking, but you're a big girl. You can decide for yourself."

She couldn't tear her gaze from him. Look at that face, she marveled silently. Look at those eyes and that nose and that mouth. "Can I?"

A small muscle pulled in his square jaw. "Oh, you do like fire, don't you?"

Her heart thumped slow and hard. "Depends on the fire. I'm pretty particular."

"You mean picky?"

She grinned. "That, too."

"So, is it a little red wine, or no wine?"

"No wine." She paused. "I don't need it with you."

"Well then, we'll have to see if I can't please you."

She could still hear his words ring in her head as he disappeared into the kitchen for the steaks. *We'll have to see if I can't please you.*

Eve smiled. Some women might not appreciate a good innuendo, but she did. Being with Zane was sexy and intense, but it could also be playful. *Fun.* It was great to feel this way around a man. It seemed forever since she was crazy in love.

Crazy in love.

Straightening, Eve glanced at the back door and then out at the barbecue with the glowing coals. But she wasn't in love...was she? This had to be a crush, infatuation, lust—something other than love.

She didn't fall in love. She was thirty-five, a die-hard realist, and the least romantic woman she'd ever known. Yet Zane made her feel things she hadn't known she was capable of feeling.

So what was happening? And where was her single-minded focus? Not on career. But Zane.

All she could think about was how much she wanted to be with him. She was practically consumed with wanting...longing. As if she'd become a lovesick thirteen-year-old all over again, struggling beneath the weight of that first crush. That all-important first love.

The door opened and Zane appeared, balancing a platter with seasoned steaks and foil-wrapped potatoes in one hand and a glass of iced tea in the other. "Close the door for me, would you?" he asked as he handed her the iced tea.

She did, and watched him head down the steps, his jeans outlining his muscled thighs and tight backside. If he looked like that in clothes, he'd be unbelievable naked.

She took a sip from her iced tea. It was sweet, tangy with lemon juice. "You remembered," she said, moving down the steps to join Zane at the barbecue.

He looked up from the grill. "What's that?"

"I like it sweet. Tart but sweet."

He shrugged. "Not hard to remember. You want your tea like your men—tart but sweet."

Eve's eyebrows arched and she grinned at him. You know, she really liked this guy.

CHAPTER TEN

DINNER WAS DELICIOUS. They ate outside on the wooden picnic table, the stars glowing bright overhead, and afterward, Eve gathered the plates and loaded the dishwasher before filling the kitchen sink with hot water for the pots and pans.

Zane carried in the rest of the dishes, and with the back door propped open, listened to the water splash as Eve scrubbed away at the pans while he wiped off the picnic table. It was the most normal sound in the world—very basic, very domestic—and yet it was strange in his kitchen. In his house.

His house without Jenny.

Slowly he wiped the crumbs off the table, letting them fall into the grass. Tonight was the first time he'd entertained a woman here since...since...

Years, he realized, not wanting to admit the truth. He hated thinking too far back, hated dwelling on what he'd lost. Because he had been happy. He'd been very happy.

When he set the empty steak platter on the counter, Eve looked up and smiled. "Thanks." A wisp of blond hair fell across her eyelid.

Without thinking, he reached out and brushed the tendril of hair away. Her smile faltered for a second and then returned. "Thanks," she said.

He hadn't meant to touch her, and yet he couldn't

seem to keep his hands to himself. Everything in him wanted her. Wanted to feel her again to see if what he'd experienced that night at McCornick and Weston's was true.

Ever since he'd danced with her, he'd wanted her back in his arms. But that was dangerous thinking. Eve wasn't a romantic and he wasn't about to fall in love. He couldn't. He'd been down that road before and it ended in a very bad place, a place he couldn't ever go again.

Yet there was something sweet about Eve at the sink, something simple and easy in the rolled-up sleeves of her shirt and the tiny white bubbles clinging to her wrists. She bent her head as she ran the scrub brush over the platter he'd brought her, her blond hair tied back in a small ponytail, exposing the graceful curve of her neck.

Platter clean, she rinsed it off and set it to dry on the towel spread on the counter.

"You're good," he said as she pulled the stopper from the sink and let the water drain.

"Years of practice," she answered, throwing a smile at him over her shoulder.

His gut tightened. It was such a genuine smile, a smile that glimmered in her eyes, as well. There were no games with this woman. No pretense, either.

And it hit him like a two-by-four in the back. *I could be happy with her.*

"Where does this go?" she asked, buffing the water pitcher dry and turning to face him.

The crystal pitcher caught the light and reflected it in streaks of red and blue and green. "Here," he said, reaching for it, his fingers wrapping over hers.

He heard her quick intake of breath and felt a hot,

electric sensation rip through him. Zane took the pitcher from her hand, set it on the counter behind him and tilted her chin up to him. She looked so serious, her blue eyes wide, fixed on his.

"Eve," he said, cupping her cheek. "It is so easy to like you."

She tried to smile, but the smile didn't reach her lovely eyes. "You make that sound like a travesty."

"I shouldn't, should I?" he answered, stroking her cheek, savoring the feel of her. She was so warm and sweet and soft, nothing like the cool, tough director he saw with the others. As he caressed her cheek again, her mouth quivered, and he stared at her lips in fascination.

"No," she whispered. "I'm a good catch."

He loved the shape of her mouth, the fullness of her lips. The upper lip was slightly bowed, the color so pink he craved a taste, desperate to see if she tasted as good as she looked. It'd been so long since he'd kissed a woman. He wasn't even sure he'd remember how.

"You're confident."

"Have to be around you," Eve answered with a slight twitch of her lips, and suddenly he couldn't resist her mouth any longer.

He hadn't wanted anything this bad in years. Lowering his head, he ever so gently touched her lips with his.

Her mouth was even softer than it looked. He didn't rush the kiss. It had been so long since he'd been this close to a woman that he wanted to savor it. He'd forgotten how sexy just a kiss could be. Forgotten that a face could be so sensitive and a mouth create so much pleasure and desire.

God, she was lovely. She felt lovely, and as the pressure of his mouth increased, her lips trembled before finally parting beneath his. With the tip of his tongue he touched her upper lip, and felt everything in him tighten with hunger.

He'd forgotten everything, he thought, exploring her upper lip with his tongue. Forgotten how much women loved to be kissed, and how a slow, sexy kiss turned up the heat faster than anything else.

She gasped at the erotic play of his tongue against her lips and her mouth parted for him inviting him inside, where it was warm and damp and oh, so sensitive. She did have a great mouth, and she was stunningly responsive. Zane fought his hunger, battled his need down to concentrate on Eve.

He'd waited so long to touch her, and even longer to let himself feel again. Now that he had, he didn't want the moment to end. He loved the taste of her, loved the way she gasped at the hot, intense sensations of their mouths and skin coming together.

She was breathing faster, her chest rising and falling with short, shallow gulps of air, and he slid his hand from her cheek to her jaw, his long fingers spanning the smooth skin. He could feel her pulse beat wildly beneath his fingertips, feel the heat grow beneath her satiny skin, and then her body curved into him.

She was seeking him out now, and the brush of her full breasts against his chest made him groan deep in his throat. He settled a hand on her lower back, urging her closer, bringing her hips in direct contact with his.

Eve made a sound that was almost a whimper, and that soft moan nearly pushed him over the edge. He felt himself harden again, his heart racing, blood pounding. His palm moved from her back to the curve of her bottom, and he couldn't believe how good she felt. He drank in her taste, and suddenly wanted to taste all of her, feel all of her, to answer the driving hunger for her heat and warmth and softness.

He wanted to bury himself in her, to fill the loneliness and emptiness that had been part of him so long. Too many years of being alone, too many years without touch—

The back door banged open and footsteps sounded. "Oh, hey! Sorry, mates."

It was Ty.

With a muttered curse, Zane set Eve aside and ran a hand through his hair. "Not a problem," he said evenly. "I need to check on the horses and lock up."

ZANE DIDN'T REALLY NEED to check on the horses. He'd checked on them earlier and they were fine. The problem was, *he* wasn't fine. He felt more than a little frustrated and very crazy.

Leaning against the corral in the dark, Zane shook his head, wishing he could clear the fog from his brain. His thoughts were so tangled that he felt like a calf tripped up by a rope.

Kissing Eve…it'd been…wow. Amazing. Perfect. And there was no way in hell he'd be able to keep his distance from her now. She felt too good in his arms. Her soft mouth tasted too fresh. She was warm like sunshine and sweet like Bing cherries.

God, he wanted her. He wanted her so badly that even now he felt the hunger in every bone and muscle of his body.

He'd only ever felt like this once before in his life, and that was with Jenny, the woman he loved. The woman he'd married.

But now he was falling for Eve, falling hard, and he knew what he wanted to do. Marry her. Make love to her. Make babies with her. He couldn't help it. He was an old-fashioned guy. Love meant marriage and babies. Lots of babies, maybe even twins, like him and Zach.

Zane shook his head in disgust. Who was he kidding? Eve wasn't going to give up her career. She wasn't going to settle down and make pies and quilts and babies.

She wasn't like his mom, for heaven's sake. Or Jenny.

She was Eve Caffrey. Hollywood.

Yet it was a little late to remember the Hollywood part. Eve had turned a switch back on, made him feel real and alive and full of emotions. Full of need, too.

Closing his eyes, Zane tried to remember life with Jenny. He tried to remember how it'd felt with her in his arms. Jenny had been sweet, they'd been good together, but the passion he felt now was something altogether new.

Despite his best efforts, he couldn't remember Jenny's touch or kiss. He could only feel Eve, and he felt her in his arms right now, felt Eve's slender body pressed against him, her soft, full breasts crushed beneath his chest, her rounded hips cradled by his.

Tonight when he'd held her, he'd wanted her so much that it made him completely lose his head.

He'd wanted her not just with his body, but his heart.

And that's the part that scared the hell out of him. He was going to lose again. He was going to lose another woman he loved. If not now, then soon.

It wasn't fair. He wasn't supposed to want what he couldn't have.

Zane stood still, sensing the futility, knowing there was no way their lives would ever work. He'd never be able to handle Eve's coming and going, and there was no way he could ask her to give up her career.

He winced, feeling a brutal shaft of pain. He'd loved once, and losing Jenny had nearly killed him. There was no way he'd ever handle loving and losing Eve. Better to stop it now and keep a tight hold on reality.

But his eyes burned. He hated living alone. He'd been so empty for so long, and Eve had made him start to hope....

To want.

To need.

But he couldn't, at least not with her. She made him feel the right things, but she wasn't the right woman. The right woman would be a country girl. The right woman wouldn't want to travel. The right woman would be someone he could watch over and protect right here on the Twin Bar Ranch.

EVE KNEW TY WAS WATCHING her as she moved around the kitchen, putting away the last of the glasses. She wasn't handling the shift in emotion very well. The kiss had been so intense, and then Zane abruptly walked out. Yes, they were interrupted, but why did he leave?

"Are you pleased with the way things went today?" she asked distractedly, her head still reeling.

"Yes."

After closing the upper cabinet, she dried her hands on a dish towel but didn't make eye contact with Ty.

"You're home earlier than I expected. I thought you'd headed out with some of the cast."

"I did, but I didn't feel like drinking, and I caught a ride back. The drinking's not helping my concentration. In fact, it's not helping anything."

She put the dish towel down. "I've never seen you struggle like this. You want to tell me what's going on?"

His cheek twitched and he shook his head. "Nothing. At least nothing I can tell you. There're some things I can't talk about."

"Maybe it'd help if you did."

"No."

"You might feel more comfortable—"

He made a hoarse sound, cutting her short. "Everything makes me uncomfortable right now, but it's not you, and it's not this film. It's me. But I'm going to work on it, Eve. I promise."

She remembered what Zane had said about Ty's past. She wanted to help Ty, support him, but forcing him didn't seem to be the answer. "I know you will."

Ty nodded toward the door. "Anyway, enough about me. What about you two? Things looked pretty hot in here."

"Don't start."

"He's not a redneck."

"Ty—"

"Okay." He held up his hands. "I'm going to go now and get some sleep. You should, too. You need it."

Eve was dying to crawl into bed, but Zane hadn't returned from the stable and she didn't want to go to bed without talking about what had happened between them. After saying good-night to Ty, she curled up on the sofa and fell asleep.

The pounding on the door woke her. Eve's head felt fuzzy as she sat up. She had no idea where she was. The room was completely dark, the blinds were drawn and no lights shone anywhere.

The pounding resumed. Eve staggered to her feet and bumped into something hard, banging her shin. It was then she realized she wasn't in her hotel, but at Zane's house.

The pounding on the door abruptly stopped and Eve heard voices—hushed masculine voices. Zane and Ty, it sounded like.

Still sleepy, brain definitely not sharp, Eve entered the kitchen. "What's going on? What time is it?"

"Five-thirty," Zane answered. He was dressed, clean shaven, hair combed. "Ty says we've got some visitors."

Eve went to the kitchen window and pushed aside the wooden blind. A white van with a satellite dish was parked next to the stable. "Oh, no."

"Oh, yes."

She blinked and stared outside again. The sun was just beginning to rise, a soft yellow light against a wispy blue sky. Why was a camera crew here? What did they want now? "This isn't going to work."

"Tell me about it." Ty looked grim. "I know I've been screwing up, and I'm sorry about that, but I don't need an audience. I can't handle an audience. I'm feeling enough pressure as it is."

Eve dropped the blind. "I'll get rid of them."

"They won't listen," Ty said, folding his arms across his chest. "The press is rabid."

She looked from Ty to Zane and back again. "Ty,

I don't think we have a choice. We've got to get this film in the can. You're in more than half the scenes we're scheduled to shoot today—''

"Give everyone the day off," Ty interrupted. "Everybody had to work yesterday. They're exhausted. The crew's already up in arms about working seven days straight. They'd love a day off. You know they'd be grateful and they'd work even harder Tuesday morning."

She didn't answer and Ty persisted. "I need the break, too, Eve. I don't know my lines. I need to get back into character. My head's been messed up, but I want to make things right. I'm determined to make things right."

"I have a cabin." Zane had been silent until then, busy making coffee. But now he turned to face them. "It's up in the high country. The place is pretty remote. I could take Ty there. We'd go by horseback. It's a fairly long ride. Three hours each way."

"Eve, you'll come, won't you?" Ty asked, running a hand through his thick, sun-streaked hair.

The last thing Eve wanted to do was go on a camp out with Zane. Just thinking about last night made her stomach somersault. The kiss was great, but Zane's hasty retreat confused her. Either he didn't enjoy the kiss, or he did, but had realized it was a mistake. Either way, she was going to be hurt.

"I can't take a day off," she said. "Even if we don't shoot today, I still have phone calls and production meetings—things that can't be ignored."

Ty swore a little. "Help me here, Eve. I've been damn close to a nervous breakdown and there's a lot I have to tell you, a lot you should know, but God

help me, I can't do it with a television crew following
me around.''

She battled the pressure building inside her. ''How
is one day off going to solve anything? I think you
need a lot more help—''

''Maybe,'' he interrupted quietly, his eyes dark with
emotion. ''But that's not going to be possible until this
film wraps up. So give everyone a day off. And give
me one more chance. *Please.*''

Eve felt the silence in the kitchen grow. She had to
say something, had to make a hard decision here.

Making a movie was business. This was a job. It
was about performance. Results.

Seeing a movie might be a feel-good experience,
but making one involved tough choices and hard decisions. The producers expected her to make those decisions, and so far she hadn't.

She'd been sensitive, sentimental, emotional. She'd
cared about morale on the set. She'd worried about
her actors' feelings. She'd tried to keep things positive—supportive.

At what price?

This was tearing her apart. One part of her wanted
to tell Ty that there was no way she'd give him any
more time off. She longed to remind him that he'd
been demanding and draining from the moment she
joined the project. She wanted to tell him that there
were plenty of sexy young stars out there who could
generate as much heat and energy and excitement as
he did, yet when she opened her eyes and looked at
him, she knew she couldn't.

The fact was she wouldn't fire him. Despite all the
problems on the set, he was still incredibly talented
and, more important, she believed in him.

Maybe she'd never be the big Hollywood director. Maybe she wasn't ruthless enough to become a huge success, but she'd remain true to herself. Hold fast to her values.

Ty was asking for a little more time. Her head was telling her no. Her gut was telling her yes. If she had to choose between her head and her instinct—instinct won.

"Twenty-four hours," she said. "I'll give everyone the day off, but we're filming again tomorrow morning."

Zane went out to meet the television crew down by the corral to tell them there'd be no filming on the ranch today. Instead, all work was being done on location somewhere in town.

When she saw the van speed off down the lane, Eve finished her calls to her assistants, asking them to finish notifying the cast and crew that everyone had earned a day of rest.

Phone calls completed, Eve, Ty and Zane set off on horseback, with bedrolls and saddlebags attached to each mount.

They rode in near silence the first hour as the sun rose higher in the sky. The morning light was bright and the air still cool. Dew clung to the grass, splattering them now and then as the horses picked their way across the lower pasture.

By midmorning they began to climb higher, and the undulating hills glistened yellow-green beneath the cloudless blue sky. It would be hot later, Eve thought, looking around her.

Their pace was slow, almost leisurely, and yet Eve felt the tension between her and Zane. He'd barely spoken to her today, and made little or no eye contact once they'd left the stable. His silence was beginning to anger her. If he had a problem, he should just say so. Ignoring her only made things worse.

They stopped for lunch along a tiny creek. Zane passed out the sandwiches Eve had made earlier that morning. They munched the sandwiches and shared a bag of chips, then Ty wandered away with his script.

Eve watched him throw himself down on the grass beneath a young oak tree a short distance away. "I wish I knew what was going on inside his head," she said.

Zane broke off a stalk of grass. "Like I said, he didn't go to an elite boarding school in Sydney, and he didn't attend that fancy acting program, either. He'd never been out of the Northern Territory until he was eighteen and left home for good. He's never been home since, and never spoken to his dad again."

"How do you know all this?"

"Zach did some more research for me." He reached for his thermos of lemonade. "There was an accident during a roundup when Ty was in his teens. His younger brothers got caught in the wrong place at the wrong time."

Eve sucked in a breath. "Were they badly hurt?"

Zane's jaw tightened. "They both died."

It was all beginning to make sense. Ty was drinking because he hated the role of Jack, or more correct, he hated how the role made him feel. Playing a cowboy, riding a horse, participating in a roundup—even if choreographed on film—was dredging up the worst kind of memories.

But suddenly she knew that's exactly why he'd taken the part. He'd thought he could handle it. Thought he'd be able to confront the past and win.

But it hadn't worked out that way. The monkey was on Ty's back and riding him hard.

She watched Ty read through the script and realized that everyone had a secret, everyone had stories they wouldn't share. "I wish he'd told me."

"Some people don't know how."

Like Zane. He wasn't ever going to tell her about his past, not if he didn't have to. And even though his past was keeping them apart, he'd live with the secret rather than share it.

But she couldn't accept that. She cared for him too much and couldn't accept that they didn't have a chance. "I know there's something you're not telling me," Eve said, carefully picking her words. "Something you don't want me to know."

Zane didn't say a word. He held the thermos loosely in his hands and stared out at the horizon.

"It can't be that bad, Zane. I know you. I know you're a good person. I promise I won't judge you—"

"It's time we moved on," he said, rising abruptly. "We have the hardest part of the climb ahead of us."

He'd turned and walked away toward the tethered horses. Eve's stomach knotted. She didn't get this. She didn't get him. Ignoring Ty's curious glance, she rushed after Zane and cornered him by the horses.

"Fine, don't talk about the past. Keep your big secret to yourself, but can we at least talk about last night?"

Zane packed the thermos in the saddle bag. "What about last night?"

"The *kiss*. Or have you blocked that, too?"

He shot her a sharp look. "I haven't blocked it. I

remember it perfectly.'' He tensed. ''It was...incredible.''

That threw her for a loop all over again. ''It was?''

''But I'm not going to kiss you again because this, us—we're not going to happen. This isn't going anywhere. As I already said, I'm not looking for a relationship—''

''Have I said anything about commitments?'' she interrupted hotly. ''Give me a break, Zane! I'm thirty-five. I've been around the block. I've kissed my share of men, and one kiss doesn't mean I lose my head!''

A small muscle jumped in his jaw and he glared down at her. ''I've been around the block, too, but I haven't been with a lot of women. I've never felt the need to be, and that kiss *did* mean something to me.''

They were both fuming and glaring, and Eve couldn't think of a damn intelligent thing to say. She crossed her arms over her chest and balled her fingers into fists. How could he do this to her? How could he make her feel so many intense emotions all at one time?

What did he want her to say? What was she supposed to do? Act cavalier? Play the tough, Teflon Hollywood director? Hide the fact that it was too late, that she'd already fallen for him hard?

Fortunately, Ty saved her from saying anything when he stood up and moved their way. ''Well, mates, we're off then, are we?''

Oh, they were off, all right, Eve vowed, fighting tears. She declined Zane's assistance and swung into the saddle, jamming her feet deep into the stirrups to hide her unhappiness.

She had a million things to do. Why on earth was

she playing cowgirl with Zane? Why had she even come on this trip?

But Eve didn't have any answers, and judging from the rigid set of Zane's back, she knew he wasn't going to be any help, either. It was going to be a very long day in very close quarters, she thought as the horses set off down the trail.

CHAPTER ELEVEN

EVE HAD NO IDEA JUST HOW close the quarters would be until they reached the top of the mountain and followed the faint trail around a bend. "This is it," Zane said as the trail led them into a clearing.

Sweat trickled down Eve's back and beads of moisture slid between her breasts. Shading her eyes, she stared at the ramshackle lean-to. Calling Zane's shack a cabin was like calling a rowboat a cruise ship. Behind the cabin rose a jagged mountain, with another massive mountain thrusting up behind that one.

Zane was already climbing the steps to the cabin and prying off the front door. The rusted hinges gave way and the door snapped from the frame.

Ty was walking around, inspecting the cabin and taking in the view before coming to Zane's assistance. "Do you get here often?"

Zane pulled the boards off the windows, inviting late afternoon sunlight to flood the dusty cabin. "Once every couple months. I usually stay here when I'm doing a property inspection—checking fences, ponds, making sure everything is in order."

"And you hammer boards across the door and windows every time?" Eve asked in disbelief.

"It only takes a few minutes and it keeps the bears out."

"*Bears?*"

"I think it's great." Ty was stacking the boards against the side of the cabin. "When I read the script this is exactly what I pictured. It's perfect, mate."

Zane's lips twisted. "Good. Let me finish showing you around."

Eve finally slid off her horse. "Is there more?"

Zane's boots made the bleached boards on the steps creak. "Just an old corral and an outhouse."

Outhouse. Eve silently repeated the word, staring at the tiny tilting building behind the cabin that Zane had just pointed to. The ancient outhouse looked as if it hugged the side of the mountain. One misstep there and she'd be over the edge of the cliff.

This was a mistake. This was such a huge mistake. She and Zane were hardly speaking, and then to be here, staying in a place like this...

There'd be no privacy. There wasn't any running water. She didn't see a kitchen or a bedroom or anything but a potbellied stove and a couple of squeaky cots. She'd never enjoyed roughing it, and her two summer camp experiences were among the worst memories of her life.

Suddenly, despite being horrendously stiff and sore, Eve wanted to climb back into the saddle and race down the mountain to the city life she adored.

No more stables. No more horses. No more sweaty cowboys. Or sexy cowboys, either.

"Oh, Eve," Zane said as he led the horses to the corral, "if you need to use the john, make sure you take a roll of toilet paper with you."

If she'd had a rock in her hand, she would have thrown it.

Ty had asked Eve to come along because he wanted her help, but once they arrived, he headed off by himself with his script, disappearing into the scrubby brush, and Zane didn't seem inclined to hang around, either. With the horses unsaddled and brushed down, he let them loose in the old corral before disappearing into the cabin.

Eve didn't know what to do with herself. She hadn't thought to pack a book, and she wasn't comfortable enough with the rugged terrain to set off by herself and explore.

She really didn't want time to think, either, because she'd done enough of that on the ride up. The fact was, she knew before they'd even left the ranch that Zane hadn't wanted her to come on this trip. A smart woman would have said fine, you don't want me, I don't want you. But Eve couldn't seem to do that. She remembered the old adage, if at first you don't succeed, try, try again. But there had to be limits. One had to be rational.

Yet when it came to Zane, she was anything but rational. She wanted to know him, wanted to be close to him, wanted to understand what made him tick. At first she'd told herself it was the mystery about him that attracted her, but honestly, the mystery was less compelling than his energy. His charisma. The man literally rocked her world, and when he kissed her... She'd never, ever been kissed like that before. It wasn't even technique. It was something that just felt right. No, better than right...*perfect*.

When he kissed her last night, the world had seemed perfect. He'd felt something, too. He said today it had been an amazing kiss, but that's all there'd be—just that one kiss.

Eve sighed and stretched a little, beginning to stiffen up from the ride. It was getting darker. The light was starting to fade. She could hear Zane moving around in the cabin and the rattle of pans. It sounded as if he was getting a jump start on dinner.

Her dad was the cook in her family, and a great cook, too, although he prepared mainly Polish specialties, like his famous borscht. You hadn't really lived until you'd tried Jacek Kowalski's borscht with just a dollop of sour cream on top.

There were times Eve would love to be a kid again, eating bread and butter with a bowl of her dad's borscht, listening to him talk about life in Kazimierz Dolny, his childhood home eighty miles from Warsaw. Those were the days when she was still Eva Kowalski, a skinny little girl with blond pigtails and neighbors with nothing better to do than gossip.

If only those neighbors were around now. Their clackety jaws would drop if they knew little Eva was directing heartthrob Ty Thomas in a movie produced by Hollywood's hottest studio. But they wouldn't know about her success because they wouldn't recognize her name.

It had been her dad's suggestion to change her name fifteen years ago, and it was odd that such a little thing could make such a difference. Once she became Eve Caffrey, doors started to open, and while she didn't always land the big jobs, she did get the interviews and at least a stab at the opportunities denied her father. There were times she thought a whole world lay between Eve Caffrey and skinny Eva Kowalski.

Restless, Eve left her seat on the rock and headed for the cabin. Someday soon she'd get her dad's borscht recipe and buy some real bread, a good chewy flour-dusted brown bread. Even if her name was different, she wasn't different on the inside. She'd always be Jacek's daughter. She'd always share his love for filmmaking.

Eve jammed her hands in her pockets and peered inside the cabin. Zane had built a fire in the old potbellied stove and it was smoking like crazy. "Hey," she said, fanning some of the smoke from her face. "Would you like some help?"

He straightened and faced her. "You're saying I need a fire truck?"

Eve's lips tugged. No one made her smile the way he did. He wasn't even all that funny. It was just him. She loved the way he talked, loved the way he said things. "Depends what you're trying to do. If you're making smoked turkey, you're on the right track."

"The turkey's already jerky."

There went her heart again. Silly flutters, as if she were a kid in school. It was going to kill her tonight, being near him and yet not being close. "And what goes with turkey jerky?"

"Canned chili."

He said it proudly, and she smiled even as her heart flipped over. Damn, she loved this man. "Perfect."

His gaze held hers for what seemed like forever. For a long moment he didn't speak, his hard features expressionless, yet there was so much energy between them, so much awareness and tension.

"Ever been married?" he finally said, breaking the silence.

"No," she answered, coloring slightly and tucking a strand of hair behind her ear. "You?"

"Yes."

Her eyes opened wide. For a moment her mind went blank, and her head filled with white noise. Then, little by little, thoughts started popping in. Married. Zane, married? A wife?

With all his hard edges, his impatience with social niceties, she'd pegged him as a confirmed bachelor. "You're divorced, then?"

"No."

Then if he wasn't married anymore and he wasn't divorced... Eve's lips parted, but she couldn't find her voice.

Zane filled the awkward silence. "She died—" He broke off and shook his head. "I killed her."

Eve's legs wobbled and nearly gave out. She grabbed one of the rickety wood chairs and sat down. "That's not funny."

"No, it's not." And he wasn't laughing. "I was driving. She was in the passenger seat."

Suddenly Eve heard Zach's words in her head. *There was an accident five years ago...changed him completely....* "So you didn't really kill her. It was a car accident and you were at the wheel."

"I'd had a drink. I shouldn't have been at the wheel," he bitterly retorted. "She'd be alive today if it weren't for me."

His words chilled her. Eve left the chair and paced a bit. She'd started her career staging accidents on movie sets, but a real crash had taken Zane's wife. "What happened?"

He sat down in the chair she'd just vacated. "Runaway truck." He extended his long legs and then pulled them back as if he couldn't get comfortable. "It's all kind of fuzzy, at least the part where I lost control. All I know for sure is that Jenny didn't stand a chance."

The cabin suddenly seemed too small, and the intense emotions too volatile. A lump filled her throat as Eve silently repeated his late wife's name. Jenny. A pretty name.

"It's been five years," he continued flatly, uneasy in the wobbly chair, "but sometimes it feels more like fifty. We knew each other since we were practically kids. I always thought we'd have forever."

"You still miss her."

He grew very still and fixed his gaze on the ground and a slow-moving spiral of dust. "At first it felt like someone had amputated part of me. I'd wake up at night feverish, sick. Now..." His voice faded away.

So this was what Zach meant when he said Zane had been through hell and back. She didn't know what to say. She didn't know what to feel. The man she loved had once been deeply in love with someone else and had tragically lost her. Worse, he said he'd killed her with drunk driving. But Zane didn't strike her as the careless type. He was one of the most controlled people she'd ever known.

Then she thought of last night's kiss. It had been intense. Emotional. *Real.* But he'd regretted it later. He'd lost control. Eve felt absolutely heartsick. She didn't stand a chance, did she?

"It's getting late," Zane said flatly, no emotion in his voice. He stood up and closed the stove, grabbed an empty pot and tossed it at her. "Catch."

Eve barely got a hold of the aluminum pan before it smacked her in the middle. "What's this for?"

"Water." He didn't ask if she was up for a hike, but a hike to the lake, it was. Her muscles protested at the exertion. The long ride had stiffened her up everywhere, and her jeans chafed the tender skin of her inner thighs, but the physical discomfort was nothing compared with the emotional.

She was struggling to come to terms with Zane's past. Struggling with the fact that he'd been married, and widowed, and even now, years later, was determined not to love again. At least now she knew why.

The setting sun cast long red-gold rays across the ground. "How are you holding up?" Zane asked. "Not too sore?"

"Nah, I'm tough."

His mouth twisted. "You are. For a city girl."

With the sun in her eyes, she couldn't see his expression but she heard his rueful laugh. "Not city," she corrected, trying to ignore how her heart ached. "Suburban girl."

Dusk was settling as they reached the lake. The lavender-blue twilight colored the arid landscape, and gold light reflected off the water's smooth surface. He filled the thermos with water as she filled the pan. Unexpectedly Zane reached out and touched her shoulder. "Look," he said quietly. "Over there."

She followed his outstretched arm as he pointed to the far side of the lake. And then in the heavy purple shadows she saw the deer. Not just one, but a whole herd, including a large buck, and a half-dozen does.

Eve drew in a swift breath.

While the buck stood guard, the others slowly, warily approached the lake to drink, their sleek, tan bodies shadowy in the fading light.

They crouched beside the lake until the deer began to wander off. When the buck finally leaped after the others, Eve turned to Zane. "That was lovely."

"Wait until you hear the coyotes later."

His smile was heartbreakingly tender and yet sad. Her heart knotted. "I think I like deer better."

"You're such a woman."

"You've noticed."

"I'd have to be blind not to." His crooked smile faded as he ran the pad of his thumb across her cheek, his touch gentle, making her feel tender, delicate, like a rare flower. "So damn beautiful."

Up close, his eyes had sharp flecks of yellow. The color was so pure it was like looking at a spring meadow filled with tender shoots of grass.

He cupped her cold face in his hands, warming her skin, warming her from the inside out. Eve couldn't move, or breathe. "You're not talking," Zane said.

Her throat felt so dry, her mouth parched. "Can't think of anything to say."

"You? The woman who has an answer for everything?"

She simply stared up at him, watching his head dip lower and lower until she could feel the caress of his breath against her lips and the heat of his skin.

He kissed her so lightly, fleetingly. Eve couldn't believe how badly she wanted him. "You said we couldn't kiss anymore," she said, her voice husky with a passion she couldn't hide.

"I'm having a hard time following my own rules."

"Maybe you could ease up on the rules for a bit. Just go by the seat of your pants."

He smiled wryly and trailed the tip of his finger across her neck. "If I do that, I'll lose all control."

"Control's overrated," she whispered, leaning forward and touching her lips to his.

Those lips, he thought, reaching up to caress her

cheeks, those lips were made for him. He'd never liked kissing anyone this much before.

He'd never felt this turned on by anyone before. He was dying to take her, explore her, taste her. He wanted everything from her and more.

But making love and being in love were two different things. He had to remember that. Stay focused on that.

"Look who's talking," he said flatly, tapping her once on the nose. "You love control."

She smiled, and he thought he'd never get tired of that smile, or the way her eyes crinkled at the corners. He'd love to wake up every morning with Eve next to him, love to watch her eyes open. This was bad. He was too attracted to her, felt too good around her. He'd told Eve about Jenny, thinking it would create a distance between them, but it had had the opposite effect. He felt closer to her than ever.

"We should get back," he said, standing up and drawing her to her feet. "I don't want Pretty Boy worrying." But more than that, he didn't trust himself alone with her. Just one kiss and he was craving her all over again, but he couldn't do this. Couldn't start with the hope and need. And he wasn't going to love Eve.

ZANE HADN'T BEEN KIDDING. Dinner really was jerky and canned chili. Eve didn't think she'd forget a tasty meal like that in a long time.

After they'd scraped their plates clean and rinsed them off, she took a seat by the fire Zane had built outside and wrapped a blanket around her shoulders.

"Did you get enough to eat?" he asked, shifting one of the logs with the tip of his boot.

"Plenty."

He laughed at her expression "Don't tell me you've never had canned chili before."

"I've never been a big chili fan," she said, drawing the blanket closer about her. "We didn't have it much growing up."

"What about all those football tailgates? After-ski meals?"

"No."

"No? You, the All-American Girl?"

"I wish." She chewed on her lip, wondering how much she should tell him. "I wasn't raised mainstream America. In fact, my real last name isn't Caffrey. It's Kowalski—"

"Like that crazy Polish director, the guy who did the Red-Eyed Martian flicks," Ty said, emerging from the cabin with his sheepskin coat. "I used to love those movies. Did you guys ever see them? They were so bad they were good. Classic stuff."

Eve smiled but it hurt on the inside. This was the part that hurt. "That's actually my dad. Jacek Kowalski."

"No shit," Ty said, dropping to the ground near the fire. "I grew up on those movies. Watched them over and over."

And her dad had hated making those movies, but for a number of years it was the only work he could get, and he had bills to pay. A family to feed. In Warsaw he would never have had to make cheap productions like that, but in the U.S. his accent held him back...that and his lack of connections.

"Why'd you change your name?" Ty asked, looking at her with renewed interest.

She felt Zane's gaze, followed by a wave of ambivalent emotions. Could she have accomplished what she had if she'd remained Jacek's daughter instead of striking out on her own? Or would her father's reputation have hurt her chances? She'd never know, would she?

Eyes stinging, she stared hard at her hands and fought to keep the emotion in check. "My dad wanted more for me," she said at last. "He loved this country, but he thought I could do even better...given the chance."

No one said anything for a moment, and the fire popped, crackled. Ty cleared his throat. "I hope you didn't think I was making fun of your dad—"

"No," she interrupted, really uncomfortable.

"Because I wasn't making fun. I mean, your dad was one of the reasons I fell in love with movies. I was a pretty messed-up kid and movies were my big escape. All that adventure, and all those sexy female astronauts." Ty laughed softly and shook his head. "I loved their platform boots and shiny silver jumpsuits. They were hot."

Eve smiled wryly. She'd loved the jumpsuits, too. She'd always wanted to wear one.

"Your dad's Polish," Ty persisted. "He was born in Poland, right?"

She nodded. "Emigrated when he was twenty."

"Kind of like Jack from the movie."

"Yeah." Eve shivered, feeling rather raw emotionally, and wrapped the blanket tighter around her. "It's cold."

"The clear night," Zane answered, speaking for the first time in a while. "Perfect for star gazing. And watching meteor showers."

Eve perked up. "Meteor showers tonight? Seriously?"

Zane added another log to the fire. "You were a science major in college. Was astronomy your thing?"

"Not really," she said, grateful to have something else to talk about. "Although now that I think about it, one of my all-time favorite labs was a visit to the observatory at Mount Wilson. We did some stargazing there, but I've always wanted to do more."

Ty snapped his coat closed and stretched out on the ground, using a small log to prop his head. "What time is this star show?"

Zane looked at his watch and then at the sky. "We probably won't see much until after ten. But once it starts, it'll last for an hour or more."

"Ten? What time is it now?" Ty asked.

"Eight-thirty."

"It seems later," Ty said, yawning. "I don't think I can make it. I'm beat. I'm going to sleep like a baby tonight." He looked at Zane. "Speaking of babies, don't you owe me a lullaby?"

Zane snorted, but Ty persisted. "You do, Dumas. You promised me some tunes if I made it up here without falling on my ass today, and I didn't fall, thank you very much."

"Didn't think you'd remember," Zane said.

"Not remember? I've been dying to hear you on the harmonica." Ty's eyes closed again but he was grinning. "Now play. Command performance."

Zane played ballads, starting with the old English version of Barbara Allen. The low, mournful notes on the cold starlit night with the fire crackling and popping was like magic.

It was so beautiful it was almost surreal, and Eve

thought this was what movies tried to do—create one singular moment in time where life has meaning. And clarity. A moment when life makes sense and feels right.

Eve closed her eyes and pressed her cheek against her blanket-covered arm. Zane was playing another ballad, and as he finished, she drew a rough breath. ''That was beautiful,'' she whispered.

''You're good,'' Ty said. ''You're really good. Where'd you learn to play?''

Zane shrugged and slid the harmonica back into his coat pocket. ''Taught myself when I was traveling a lot on the circuit. It was a way to pass the time.''

''You play anything else?''

''Piano. Guitar. Some fiddle. Zach plays most of them, too.''

''I bet you sing,'' Ty guessed.

''A little.''

Eve turned her head to look at Zane and her heart constricted.

Lord have mercy, she loved this man, and it wasn't a crush. It wasn't infatuation. It was love. Real love. Deep love. The kind that didn't go away.

Damn it. Look at him. He was gorgeous. And tough. But tender, too, she knew that much.

There was a lot about him to love. She loved his eyes. The most beautiful eyes she'd ever seen, and the way he walked was just plain sexy. She loved his mouth and his hands, and his touch drove her wild. But it wasn't his body or even his mind that made her crazy for him. Her feelings, this intense attraction, had nothing to do with his looks and everything to do with his heart.

Back in Hollywood it seemed that men exchanged

women as if they were cars. The men she worked with were always in the process of getting married or getting divorced or having an affair. Eve had become so jaded to it all. But Zane was different. He might not fall in love easily, but his love would be love worth waiting for.

She wrapped her arms around her knees and stared into the fire. The flames flickered red and gold, and she was suddenly really glad she'd made the long ride here. If she hadn't taken the trouble—or the risk—she'd never have this memory, and it was definitely one she wanted to keep.

Ty sat up, picked up a pebble lying near his boot and tossed it. "I changed my name, too," he said, breaking the stillness. "But I did it to spite my dad. Where I come from, everybody knows my dad, Buck. Buck Williams, there's a piece of work for you." He turned his head and looked at Eve and Zane. "Growing up, I was just one of Buck's brats. Mum died after Jamie was born, and we pretty much raised ourselves. There were three of us boys once, and now I'm the only one left."

Eve couldn't look away from the anger burning in Ty's intense blue eyes. "You know why *American Jack* was such a popular book?" he demanded. "Everybody could relate to it. Everybody knows what it's like to have a dream—to have that hungry feeling. I sure as hell did. Growing up, all I wanted was out. A chance to be someone else. To live somewhere else. And I did it."

"You're definitely someone," Eve said, knowing that Ty had gone from cast extra to star in less than five years. "You're one of the biggest names out there."

Ty stared out across the dark horizon. "I wanted this part. I really wanted this part because the story made so much sense to me. It said everything I ever wanted to say, but once we started filming, I panicked. The whole thing came rushing back. My dad. My brothers. The shit life I lived, and then losing Jamie and Bo. It was hell being the oldest, but to have the younger ones taken? If God was going to take them, he should have taken me, too."

Lifting his head, he looked at Eve, his eyes sparking in the firelight. "They were just little guys. They shouldn't have been on a roundup, but my dad was so damn cheap he'd rather put a nine- and eleven-year-old to work than hire regular hands. He put them out there, and sent me to watch over them, and it all got so fouled up."

"It happened on a roundup," Eve said.

"Yeah. The cows got spooked—I still don't know why—they started to stampede. Those boys got caught in the middle of the stampede, and I'm screaming and hollering. I'm begging them to ride out and they couldn't. Jesus!" His voice broke and he wiped his eyes. "I couldn't get to them in time. I couldn't do anything."

"I heard you tried," Zane said quietly. "I heard you fought to save them."

Ty shook his head, swallowing hard. "It should have happened to me, not them. Mum asked me to look after them, but when they needed me the most, I couldn't do a damn thing."

Eve's eyes burned. "No wonder this movie's been hell for you."

"I wasn't always afraid of horses," Ty said. "I used to be a damn good rider. I used to be friggin' tough." He wiped his eyes again and gave his head the briefest shake. "I *am* Jack. I *am* American Jack."

Zane threw a small twig into the fire and it sparked with a small gold flame. There was a long, taut silence.

"It's brutal what happened," Zane said as the silence stretched. "But you know the story has a happy ending. Jack finds what he's looking for."

Ty smiled, but the smile didn't reach his eyes and the tears continued to fall. "Not without a hell of a fight."

"I know. But isn't that the whole point of life?"

CHAPTER TWELVE

IT WAS QUIET AFTER TY went inside the cabin. The fire continued to burn, and the stars remained sharp and white, but there was a shift in mood. "He's all right," Zane said, standing up to put a log on the fire. "He's going to be fine."

"You think?" Eve answered distractedly, watching him settle back onto the ground, fascinated by the bend in his knee and the way the muscles bunched in his thigh.

"I don't just think, I know."

She was silent a moment. "He's been through so much."

"Especially at a young age. It's one thing to face something like that when you're an adult, but when you're fourteen or fifteen?" He shook his head. "But Ty's tough and he's got a good heart. He's going through a lot right now, but it might be just what he needs to put some of his ghosts to rest."

What about your ghosts? Eve wanted to ask him. When do you get to put them to rest? Instead, she kept the conversation on safe topics. She and Zane didn't need more tension tonight.

"Have you noticed that he's started to call me 'boss'?" Zane said, rolling the twig between his hands.

"That's what they call a station manager in the Out-back," she answered. "It's a sign of respect."

He shrugged. "Maybe." His expression was pensive. "Life's full of surprises, isn't it?"

She heard pain in his voice. Weariness, too. "Not all are bad, Zane."

"Didn't say they were."

"You're thinking about Jenny." She hadn't meant to say it, but somehow it slipped out.

"Ty's brothers, too. And you." His dark gaze met hers. "You've been through a lot, haven't you?"

"Hasn't everyone?"

Eve didn't like talking about her past, Zane realized, still staring hard into her eyes.

He'd seen her face when Ty mentioned Kowalski's Martian films. Fine muscles at her eyes tightened, and her upper lip trembled before she pressed her mouth together, holding in whatever it was she felt. And then when Eve had said "That's my dad," her voice betrayed everything she was feeling. Love, pride, pain.

Love for her father. Pride in his work. Pain that he'd…what? Eve had said he was still alive. Why would she feel pain when she spoke of him? "Your dad," he said carefully, "he's well?"

"Yes."

She'd smiled quickly but her expression was guarded. "You two didn't have a falling-out, did you?"

"No. We're good. He's healthy and he's working here and there, which is really good for him. It's just that he doesn't work as much as he used to, and Dad's not good at sitting around." She made a face, but she wasn't able to hide her worry. "I really wish he'd get another project. It'd be great to see him focused. Happy."

"I'm sure he's proud of you."

Eve drew a deep breath and he saw her eyes fill with sudden tears. "But you know, Zane, I'd trade my successes if it meant he could have some. I believe in him so much. I respect him so much. He came to this country with nothing and…" She couldn't finish the sentence. She shook her head, and struggled to dash the tears away with the back of her fist. "Sorry. I hate it when I do that."

He wished he could wrap her up in his arms and protect her from all the bad things in the world, but it didn't work like that. Even though he was big he wasn't infallible, and he'd learned that lesson when his stupidity took Jenny's life.

But that didn't stop him from wanting to shield Eve, to use his shoulders and body to keep fear and worry away. "You're going to make it, Eve. You're going to achieve all those dreams. I know it. I feel it."

She tried to smile but she couldn't, and her black lashes were damp, matted from her tears. "I hope so. I have to make it big so I can show my dad that everything he struggled for, everything he wanted, wasn't in vain."

"That's quite a burden."

"Not a burden." She managed a real smile this time, one with courage and conviction. "It's an honor. I'm really proud to be that crazy Polish director's daughter."

"You're an amazing woman, Eve Kowalski."

She bit her lip, trying hard to keep fresh tears from falling. "Eva."

"I like your name, Eva Kowalski. It's almost as pretty as you."

"You're making fun of me."

"Never."

His voice was so gentle that Eve had to swallow hard and count to ten to keep from crying again. She felt worn out, emotionally spent, and part of her wanted to run to him, and another part wanted to run away.

She looked up and her eyes met his. And just like that she felt the current again, the crazy sense that she and Zane were connected to the same hot wire.

She didn't understand what he did to her, but he did something, and it was potent. Intoxicating. She was feeling so much right now, and it had nothing to do with physics. This was pure emotion. All heart.

"Scoot over," he said, his eyes never leaving hers. "Sit with me."

She didn't need to be asked twice. Eve moved over and sat down next to him. As she did a bright light arced high overhead. "A meteor," she whispered in awe, craning her head to watch the complete path. It was such a brief glimpse, but dazzling nonetheless.

Zane shifted her so she sat between his legs and leaned against his chest. As another meteor shot across the sky, he wrapped an arm around her shoulders and held her close. He was so warm, and the air on her face so cold and crisp.

"This is lovely," Eve said, reaching up to hold Zane's arm. "I'm glad I'm here."

He looked down into her flushed face, seeing her bright eyes. "I'm glad you came," he said huskily. "I didn't know how this would work, but you fit here. You make it right."

She hugged his arm tighter. She didn't answer. She knew he didn't expect her to, either.

They sat for an hour like that, bodies warm, awareness heightened, and yet comfortable. *Peaceful.*

With the glittering sky overhead and the quiet night wrapped around them, Eve saw possibilities she'd never seen before. She pictured a life with Zane, splitting her time between Los Angeles and the ranch. She could fly to Reno on weekends. It was a direct flight, just a couple of hours long. There was no reason it wouldn't work. Lots of people commuted home. More and more folks in Hollywood had second homes in Sun Valley or Jackson Hole.

Eve slipped her fingers through Zane's. If everyone else jetted back and forth, why couldn't she?

Later, after walking her to the cabin door, Zane held her face between his hands and kissed her as if she were both beautiful and rare, exciting and sacred. Something happened in that kiss, in her heart, and she knew she'd crossed the bridge of no return.

She'd never forget Zane. Never not love him. Work was one thing, but it wasn't Zane.

In the cabin, as she lay sleepless on her narrow bunk bed, the enormity of it all hit Eve again.

She'd fallen in love with Zane and she didn't want to leave him, didn't want to imagine a future without him. She knew she would never feel this way about anyone else. It had only taken her thirty-five years, but she'd finally found the person who made her feel like herself. Like Eva.

That was the craziest part of all. Falling in love hadn't made her want to run away from her life, or stop working, or give up her dreams. It just made her more aware. Made her begin to think about other things in life, areas she'd ignored or neglected.

Like family.

Before she'd met Zane, she'd never really thought about children, but there was something about Zane that made her crave permanence and stability. Eve pressed her hands against her flat belly and imagined what it would be like to have a baby with Zane. To carry his child, to see Zane's eyes or smile in their infant's face.

She'd never understood the desire to recreate one's love until now. But loving Zane changed everything.

THE DAWN BROKE CLEAR and bright and they spent fifteen minutes closing up the cabin, then were on the trail, heading back home.

They reached Twin Bar Ranch just a few minutes after nine—and a little over three hours in the saddle. Eve barely had time to run a comb through her hair and put on a change of clothes before they started filming.

The clear morning gave way to a darkening afternoon, and by the time they wrapped up the scenes they were scheduled to shoot, heavy rain clouds blanketed the horizon.

Eve was still in discussion with her executive staff when the first cool, fat raindrops fell. Within ten minutes the rain was pelting everyone and everything, but Eve hardly felt it. Despite the late start, it had been one of their most productive days yet. Ty was on. The crew was relaxed. The cast needed little or no prompting. All in all it had been an outstanding day.

Eve passed Zane on her way to the house. "You're

drenched,'' he said, taking in her dripping blouse and slacks.

"It's coming down pretty hard."

"Why don't you go take a hot bath? You've earned it."

She pushed back a handful of wet hair. She was sopping wet, but she felt so damn good right now, she really didn't mind. "What about dinner? Don't you want me to get something started? I know they don't deliver pizza out here."

He laughed. "No, they don't, but it's all right. I've got a mess of frozen meals, thanks to my sister Melinda. I'll stick something in the oven once I finish up in the barn. You go on inside. I don't want you to catch cold. You can't afford to get sick."

He told her to use his bathroom, since it had the only tub in the house, and gave her instructions for finding some plush new towels. The linen closet was actually a closet in one of the spare bedrooms.

Eve dripped her way through the house, down the hall and to the far wing of bedrooms, turning on lights as she went, fantasizing about taking a hot bath in a huge cast-iron bathtub. *With Zane.* Now, there was a tantalizing thought!

The first room was her guest bedroom and the last was Zane's, so Eve opened the door in the middle and flipped on the light. She stopped short inside the door.

There was no bed in this room. No dresser or nightstand, no pictures on the wall. The room, just a door away from Zane's bedroom, was empty except for a long worktable and a simple wood stool. On the corner of the table stood a round plastic container, rather like a tall lazy Susan, filled with pens and brushes.

Curious, Eve walked to the table and picked up one

of the soft brushes. Many of the studio animators used
pens and brushes like these. It was odd to see the
worktable and art supplies here. Who painted? Zane
was a talented musician, but art? Maybe it was Melinda's.

Or Jenny's?

Feeling like an outsider, Eve slipped the brush back,
wiped her damp hand on the back of her even damper
jeans, and headed for the closet. She just wanted her
towel and bath.

The closet door was already a little bit ajar, but there
were no shelves of sheets and towels inside the closet,
just stacks of identical cardboard boxes. The closet
was literally lined from floor to ceiling, and the boxes
looked brand-new.

Eve couldn't explain her curiosity, or her dread. She
had no business being here. This obviously wasn't the
linen closet and she knew Zane hadn't meant to send
her here, but she couldn't just walk out. The boxes
fascinated her in a rather morbid kind of way.

Heart thudding, she reached for one of the boxes on
the top. It definitely wasn't empty. As she lifted it
down, she heard a clink inside. Removing the lid, she
reached down and pulled out a mug protected with
bubble wrap.

She pushed aside more bubble wrap and found another mug. All in all the box held eight mugs, each
featuring a whimsical hand-painted design.

Reaching out, she pressed against the tower of
boxes, causing it to sway a little. When she heard a
clink clink, clink, she realized that every box was filled
with the same thing.

For a long moment Eve couldn't move, trying to
imagine what the painted mugs were for. Then know-

ing she'd overstepped the boundaries of hospitality,
she put the box away and gently shut the door.

Chin deep in the bath, the water deliciously hot, Eve
tried to put the mugs out of her mind but wasn't completely successful.

They were probably Melinda's. Zane had told her
Melinda and her children had lived at the ranch for a
while. Or maybe Zane made knickknacks on the side.
They were beautiful mugs. Art galleries and boutiques
would love them. Heck, she'd love one. She'd have to
ask Zane about it later.

Eve was still soaking when she heard a knock at
the bathroom door. "Did you find the towels?" It was
Zane.

"Yes, thanks. I grabbed two."

"Need anything else?"

A thought came to mind, but she doubted he was
game. "You could join me."

The bathroom door slowly opened and Zane stood
in the doorway, leaning against the painted frame.
"But I already showered."

So he had. And he was wearing nothing but old gray
sweatpants that hung on his lean hips, exposing very
sexy hipbones and the hard cuts in his abdomen.

Washboard abs. Perfect pecs. Wow. "You look
clean," she said, praying for self-control.

"I am."

Eve felt a little less guilty giving him the once-over
because he was doing the same to her, and from the
frank admiration in his eyes, she knew he liked what
he saw. "Warm enough?" she asked.

The corner of his mouth lifted. "You don't think I
should be?"

He really was close to irresistible. "I wasn't sure if

this is how you usually dress, or if you're showing off for me.''

His smile made his green eyes dance. "And what would I be showing off? My embarrassing lack of chest hair?''

Eve laughed out loud. "You have a perfect chest and you know it. Stop fishing for compliments. Now, either come in or go out, but please shut the door.''

He came in and closed the door behind him. "So what do I do now?''

"Considering you're not exactly a teenager anymore, you're really rather hopeless.''

"Hopeless.''

"Mmm, that or a tease.''

"I object.'' Zane moved toward the tub and leaned over to test the temperature with his fingers. "You're the one who can't go anywhere alone. Every time I try to make a move on you, Mr. Heartthrob's there.''

Eve grew warm as his gaze skimmed the water's surface. She knew he could see the swell of her breasts above the few remaining bubbles and the paleness of her skin below, and while she'd never considered herself daring before, she loved the way he was looking at her. "Well, he's not here now.''

Zane crouched next to the tub and with one hand drew invisible patterns in the water. "I never get tired of looking at you. You're so beautiful. Wet, dry, on a horse, in the tub, it doesn't matter. You take my breath away.''

She blushed faintly. "Thank you.''

He tipped his head, studying her. "I bet your mom's beautiful, too.''

"She is pretty. She's a makeup artist. Met dad on the job.''

"They're still together?"

"Forty years this year."

He reached out and swept a damp tendril from her cheek, tucking it behind her ear. "Do you think they're happy?"

"You mean, still?" she asked, and saw him nod. Her parents weren't like most people. They had such a sense of purpose. From the beginning her mother believed in her father's vision, had shared the same dream. It was inspiring, as well as intimidating. "Yes. I think so."

She captured his hand, her fingers entwined with his. "And your parents?"

His features tightened briefly, then eased. "Still together."

"Are they having trouble?"

His fingers squeezed hers. "No. They're fine. I think I'm still trying to get used to the idea that they're not my parents biologically."

"You and Zach were adopted?"

"Sort of." His brow creased. He looked decidedly uncomfortable. "We were switched at birth."

Eve leaned toward him. "Is that possible?"

He shrugged but didn't speak, and she didn't, either. Zane certainly had a lot on his plate. His whole world was rocked five years ago and just kept on rocking.

After a minute he lifted her hand, kissed her wet palm. "Will you let me do something?"

Eve looked up, her eyes meeting his, and she felt her heart jump. Lord have mercy, she loved this man. "What?"

"Just say yes."

Her cheeks grew hot. There went her imagination again. It was crazy how much she wanted him, how much he turned her on. "Yes." She leaned even closer and kissed his mouth. "What am I saying yes to?"

"I'm going to wash your hair."

Eve chewed on the inside of her lip as she watched him work the golden shampoo between his big hands, little by little transforming the pale liquid into white, foamy lather.

She couldn't quite believe he really wanted to do this, but once he drew her back against the tub and began to massage the shampoo into her hair, she knew she had an expert on her hands. He had the best touch in the world.

Eyes closed, she felt herself relax as he worked the herbal-scented lather into her hair, creating bubbles that cascaded down her neck and onto her bare shoulders.

She felt his fingertip slide down her neck as he caught streaking suds, and she sighed with pleasure when he resumed the scalp massage, fingers and knuckles working as if he were a professional masseuse. "Damn, you're good with your hands."

"The horses say the same thing."

Grinning, Eve opened one eye and looked up at him. "The horses? Which horses?"

"All of them. This is horse shampoo, you know. It's good stuff, too. Only the best for you." Suddenly his head dipped and his mouth captured hers in a long, slow, sweet kiss, a kiss that sent shivers racing up her spine and desire coiling in her belly.

When his hand cupped her breast and spread the sudsy lather across her nipple, Eve tingled and ached. She caught his hand and held it tightly against her, almost overwhelmed by her love and need. She wanted him physically, but sex was just a small part of it. She wanted all of him, his body, his warmth, his heart—*him.*

"You're driving me crazy," she whispered.

"We can't have that," he answered, turning the faucet back on to rinse her hair. "Let's get you clean."

Satisfied he'd washed all the shampoo suds out, Zane pulled the plug on the drain in the tub, reached for a towel and carefully blotted her damp face dry. "You're staying the night—with me?"

It was less question than statement, and when Eve nodded agreement, Zane motioned for her to stand. Water streamed from her body as she shyly got to her feet. His eyes traveled the length of her, seeing everything, missing nothing, taking particular interest in her rosy-tipped breasts and the dark blond curls between her thighs.

A tiny muscle jumped in his jaw, and moving with purpose, he wrapped her in the oversize bath towel and swung her into his arms. He didn't stop moving until he placed her in the center of his bed.

"Is this what you want?" he asked, his voice deep, almost strained.

Her heart pounded. "Yes."

"Because if it's not, I want you to get your clothes and make your escape."

Eve sat up on her knees and let the towel fall. She was completely naked in the middle of his bed, and for the first time in her life, she was completely without inhibition. Leaning forward she reached out to him and tugged once on the drawstring of his sweatpants. "I want these off."

She helped slide the gray cotton sweats off his lean

hips and felt a small thrill when she saw he was already very aroused. "You don't like me, do you?"

He joined her on the bed, gently pushing her backward. "Not at all."

CHAPTER THIRTEEN

SHE'D NEVER BEEN MORE ready to make love, and when Zane parted her knees with his and opened her thighs to enter her body, Eve drew a ragged breath. She felt as if she'd waited for him all her life. She'd had sex, climaxed, tried different positions, but it had all been activity, never love.

Never love until now, and she knew it was love when he entered her, his body hard and hot and filling her completely. She closed her eyes, wrapped her arms around his neck. "Nothing fancy," she whispered. "Just hold me. Be with me."

It was slow, old-fashioned, utterly heart-melting lovemaking. As he buried himself in her, she could feel her warm, satiny skin covering muscle, smell the clean scent of his skin, and taste him with each kiss. He had such a powerful body, and yet he was tender, careful, attuned to Eve's needs.

"Is this what you want?" he asked as he slowly withdrew, nearly pulling out, only to thrust more deeply inside.

It was hard to think, hard to talk when he was giving her such incredible pleasure. Just the feel of him inside her made her feel wanted. Needed. Loved.

He continued to move inside her, each thrust steady, deep, his weight supported on his elbows. She loved the rasp of his chest against her breasts, the feel of his thighs between hers and the way he sucked the tip of her tongue, heightening the sensation of his body filling hers.

The pressure was building inside her womb and it became consuming. Each powerful thrust pushed her a little higher, made her feel a little more, craving increased contact. The more he gave her, the more she wanted, and the more she wanted to give back to him.

She felt so close to him they could have shared the same skin, and his body felt like heaven. He was so strong, so good with her. He touched her the way she'd always wanted to be touched, and as she kissed him, she sensed herself beginning to lose control, muscles tightening, pulse quickening, her body gripping him deep inside her.

She could hardly focus anymore, and with each thrust of his hips, he was pushing her up, up to the point of no return. Just before she hit it, she held him tight and whispered, "I love you...I love you, Zane...I love you," and as he buried himself inside her one last time, she came. But Zane didn't come inside her. He made sure he pulled out.

"I'm on the pill," she said later, when she'd caught her breath and managed to find her voice again.

"I wasn't sure, and I didn't want to ruin the moment."

She smiled a little, and turning her face against his chest, she kissed the warm skin of his shoulder. "It was quite a moment."

"It was all right?"

"It was the best." She lifted her head, looked down at him. "You are the best."

His mouth curved faintly. "I'm out of practice. It's been a while."

She traced his beautiful mouth. She loved his mouth. But then, she loved everything about him. "How long is a while?"

"Try five years."

Five years. Incredible. Not that he'd gone so long without sex, but that he'd needed five years to come to terms with the loss of his wife.

She snuggled closer to him and sighed with pleasure when he wrapped an arm around her, holding her against him. It wasn't sex, she thought. This was love, and making love had never felt more right in all her life.

It had been amazing being part of him, connected to him—the most beautiful thing she'd felt in her life. All those movies she'd rejected as corny...all those scripts she'd passed up because of the implausible love story...they suddenly made sense.

Her eyes grew heavy and her body felt languorous, sated. With a sigh, she gave herself up to the feeling and let sleep claim her.

Zane leaned on his elbow and gazed down at sleeping Eve. Damn, damn, damn. It had happened. Not sex. *Love.* He loved her.

He ran a finger down a tendril of her hair, the pale blond strands silky gold against the white pillow. Asleep, she looked so young, almost like a kid. How different from the daytime, when she stuck her chin in the air, braced her shoulders and took on the world with her cool, cocky attitude of *Is that the best you can do?*

She was brave. She was beautiful. But she wasn't infallible. One day she'd meet her match, or worse. One day she'd get knocked flat, and she wouldn't even know what hit her.

His chest felt tight and he drew a slow painful breath. He couldn't bear to see her hurt. Couldn't bear to lose her. He'd loved Jen, and they'd had a good life together, but what he was feeling for Eve staggered him. It also scared the hell out of him.

Lightly, very lightly, he touched her smooth cheek. His love for her was like a fire in his heart, and the fire burned hot now.

He'd known that making love to her would be powerful, but it had been far more intense than he expected. Holding her, feeling her heart beat beneath him, absorbing the soft heat of her body as he entered her made him realize how much he loved her, how much he needed her, and how difficult it would be to let her go.

Eve sighed in her sleep and turned toward him, instinctively creeping closer until her breast brushed his forearm. She felt so warm and smelled so sweet. He could still remember the taste of her on his tongue, feel the way her body welcomed him, held him. It had been amazing.

It still felt amazing. The fact that she could make him hope and feel and believe…who would have thought it possible?

EVE OPENED HER EYES SLOWLY and spotted Zane lying next to her. She turned to see him better and discovered he was awake. "What time is it?"

"Almost five."

She yawned and nestled her cheek deeper into the down pillow, savoring the cozy warmth. "It's early."

"I'm just about to get up."

"You've got to be kidding."

He laughed softly. "No, and you're going to have

to get up soon, too. You're back at work today, remember?"

"Yes, but the crew won't be here for two hours," she answered, pushing the pillow away and reaching out for him. "So that gives us at least one more hour in bed."

His mouth curved as he lifted her up and settled her on top of him. "And what did you have in mind?" he asked, touching her cheek with the back of his hand, his finger caressing her skin as if it was the softest thing he'd ever felt. "Sixty more minutes of sleep?"

His eyes looked bottle green in the dark and she felt a flicker of desire. It was happening again. The craving to be held by him, loved by him. "Maybe we could talk."

He slowly outlined her mouth. "Is that what you want? Words?"

She pressed her palms to his chest. His muscles were hard and sleek beneath warm skin. "You've a better idea?"

He didn't immediately answer, still intently tracing her mouth, and Eve's senses screamed for relief as heat raced through her—heat, hunger…and honey. She drew a tremulous breath, his touch making her tremble from head to toe, her longing so intense that she ached for him to take her, ached for his hardness and strength.

Suddenly she didn't feel like playing, or teasing. Her gaze met his, and she watched his eyes darken, the green irises turning stormy.

"I don't think I could ever get tired of waking up with you," she said huskily. "It feels so right."

"I've been thinking the same thing," he said, lowering her head to his.

"Good." Her eyes fluttered closed as desire curled like a spring in her belly. "Let's definitely talk about this, but can we wait until later today? There's something else more urgent."

"Yes, I'm feeling it, too." His mouth captured hers in a kiss that was neither brief nor tentative. This kiss was a kiss of possession. He parted her lips and savored the softness of her mouth, tasting, exploring, setting every nerve ending on fire.

He was good, so good, and he just made her want more. Sighing, Eve wrapped her arms around his neck, pressing her breasts against his chest. She felt him harden yet again, his body thrusting against her, answering the fever raging beneath her skin. A fever that only Zane could soothe.

THEY WERE BACK ON SCHEDULE, Eve thought fourteen hours later as the last of the crew headed home for the night. The day had gone well, very, very well, although Eve had had her doubts earlier that morning when Hugh Armstrong, Eve's pick for a stunt double, arrived on the ranch with his fiancée, Kate Cooper, a well-known photographer from the East Coast who specialized in glamour and high-fashion shoots.

When Hugh introduced Eve to Kate, he mentioned that Kate was interested in doing a photo shoot on the ranch, and he hoped Eve would give Kate a chance to pitch her project. Eve's guard immediately went up. She'd worked with Hugh a number of times and really liked him, but she wasn't at all sure she had time, or energy, to accommodate one more person's agenda.

Yet Kate was terrific, quickly putting Eve at ease.

"Please don't feel as if there's any pressure," she said
with a warm smile. "The project just came up. A magazine fashion editor I work with heard I was heading
this way and thought it'd be great to get shots of Ty
in some designer wear posed against a western back-
drop. But I made no promises. I'm really flexible, and
it's entirely up to you."

Eve couldn't argue with that. "Well, the layout does
sound interesting, and if Ty and his agent agree, and
if we can work the shoot around our film schedule, I
don't see why it couldn't happen."

Introductions over, it was time to get down to work,
and they did. It was remarkable, Eve thought, what a
difference a few days could make. The cast and crew
were extremely focused. Ty knew his lines and per-
formed flawlessly, nailing three scenes that morning
in just one or two takes. The weather even cooperated
with the storm clouds blowing out and leaving a baby-
blue sky.

Hours sped by as if they were nothing, and Eve
worked straight through without stopping for lunch.
The crew only quit when the setting sun forced them
to call it a day.

As cast and crew headed for the cars that would
carry them back to Reno, Eve was really pleased with
all they'd accomplished and looked forward to resum-
ing work in the morning. Days like today, when everything clicked, she was nuts about her work, just
incredibly passionate. These were the days when she
knew she couldn't do anything else. Making movies
was what she loved. And it was what she did best.

Zane was waiting for Eve on the steps of the house.
"Didn't think you were ever going to finish," he
drawled, really glad to see her. She'd been away from

him—what? All of twelve hours? But it seemed more like twelve days. "How'd it go?"

"Great." She grinned and stretched, happy as a kid on Christmas morning. "Today was one of those rare days where everything went like clockwork."

As she stretched, a soft wave of hair brushed her cheek, half hiding one of her blue eyes, and his body tightened. Eve was too good to be true. She'd brought him back to life, made him feel again, made him dream. Maybe there was a way for them to make this work. Maybe she could be happy here, living on the ranch with him.

He could see it all now—horses, dogs, kids, a big family. He already had the house with the stable and the big split-rail fence. Now all he needed was Eve and a baby or two.

It could work, he thought, and he felt a welling of tenderness. She felt right here on the ranch with him. She made this cold, empty house feel like home.

"Well, it gets better," he said. "I've even got a hot dinner waiting."

Her smile slipped. "Oh, Zane, I wish I could join you, but we've got a director's meeting in less than an hour at the hotel in Reno. I need to freshen up and head straight in."

It's not a big deal, he told himself. She had a meeting, and he hadn't cooked anything fancy. But he hated the hot rush of emotion, hated the intensity of it.

"No problem." He managed a casual shrug. "What time will you be back tonight?"

"Late. Ten, eleven. It depends how everything goes." She closed the distance between them, stood on tiptoe and kissed him. "Where do you want me to sleep when I get back? The guest room or—"

"My room," he finished. "In my bed."

But as Eve headed for Reno twenty minutes later, he felt a wave of disappointment and a keen sense of loss. He didn't want her to go. Didn't like that she had a meeting this late. She'd already put in a twelve-hour day. Why did she have to head out at night?

It's her job, he answered himself, pulling the taco casserole from the oven and setting it on the stove. Being a director wasn't a regular nine-to-five job. It was unpredictable, demanding, consuming, and she was only here at the Twin Bar because of her job. When the movie wrapped, she'd be off somewhere else.

She could be back, though. There were lots of flights from L.A. to Reno. She could come in on weekends....

Weekends. He could just see himself waiting all week to see her. They'd have a day or two together, and then she'd be gone again. His gut knotted. What kind of life was that?

He stopped himself. Don't jump ahead, don't think too much. Keep it easy. Remember to take it one day at a time. Eve's not going anywhere for a while. You've got the next month. Four weeks. Enjoy it while it lasts.

THEY ESTABLISHED A ROUTINE over the next couple of weeks. Even if they didn't go to bed at the same time, they always woke early and made love before they started the day. That quiet hour in the morning was their time. Sometimes their lovemaking was slow and tender, and other times fiercely physical, but it always brought them together, helped them grow closer.

After making love, Zane started the coffee and would step into the shower as Eve stepped out. Sometimes if she lingered in the shower, he'd join her beneath the hot spray and then they'd really be late, forced to chase down toast with gulps of hot coffee.

Eve loved the mornings best. They were warm, private, intimate. Being with Zane centered her, made her feel smart and funny and capable. She loved waking up each morning, loved anticipating the day.

"How's it going on the set?" Zane asked, busy shaving, his jaw and neck lathered with foam. They'd spent so long in bed this morning they had to drink their coffee in the bathroom, sharing counter space. Eve had managed to get panties and a bra on, but Zane still only had a towel wrapped around his hips.

"Great," Eve answered, reaching for her coffee cup. "Ty's so on it's almost scary."

It wasn't until she put the big mug down that she remembered she'd been meaning to ask Zane about the boxes of similar mugs in the closet and the room with all the art supplies.

"These mugs are really fun," Eve said, running the pad of her thumb over the whimsical western design.

Zane rinsed his razor. "Jen painted them."

"She was an artist, then?"

His shoulders shifted. "She dabbled in art. She was always working on something. Her dream was to get her work in some of the local galleries."

Eve studied the ranch emblems on the mug. Hers had a black horseshoe. Zane's had a red bucking horse. "It didn't work out?"

Zane glanced down at his cup and swallowed hard. "No."

They were so alike, Eve thought, sensing the struggle within him. He hated talking about Jen just like she hated talking about her past. For her, it was the lingering shame she felt that people had ridiculed her father. But Zane's past was so much harder…so much darker. Yet instead of moving on, he was still living here, in this house, surrounded by the life he'd once shared with his wife.

ALTHOUGH SHE WAS WORKING long hours, Eve had never been happier. A week had passed, and she couldn't hide her smile of satisfaction at all they'd accomplished.

She was pleased—no, make that totally jazzed—about the scene they'd just shot. Ty and Bethany, Ty's female co-star, nailed the emotions the first time, but this, the fifth take, was by far the best—real anger, real frustration, really great acting. "Perfect," she said, getting up from her chair. "You guys got it. Thank you. We're moving on now. Next scene."

The cast relaxed and broke into chatter as the crew immediately began repositioning the equipment, moving the cameras and lights around to frame the corral.

Eve glanced up at the sky as she thought ahead to the next scene. The lighting so far was perfect. They'd had sunshine all morning, and it looked as if it would continue into the afternoon.

Her gaze swept from the endless blue horizon to the corral, and Eve spotted Zane off to the side, waiting for her. It was the first time she'd seen him since breakfast and she headed in his direction. "Good morning, stranger."

"I'd say good morning but I think it's almost afternoon," he answered. He was wearing a crisp western-style shirt, boots and dark, fitted Wrangler jeans.

He looked rugged, handsome, and she couldn't believe he was hers. Well, almost hers. "Where are you going?"

"Town. I'm meeting Melinda and Kerry for lunch."

Eve felt a prick of envy. She'd love to be heading to town for lunch with Zane and his sisters. "So when are you going to introduce me to the other women in your life?"

"Once I know you plan on sticking around awhile." He was smiling. Barely.

For the first time she felt a strange undercurrent of tension between them, and not the good kind. "Zane, I'm practically living with you."

"You're halfway through the production schedule."

"We're making great progress, but what does that have to do with you and me?"

He looked away, his expression blank. "Ty said you've got another project lined up. You're scheduled to start work overseas in a couple of months."

"And?"

"You live on the road, don't you?"

Eve glanced over her shoulder at her crew. They were almost ready for her. "This is my job. This is what I do. But I have breaks between films. I have an apartment in Westwood. I do have a regular life, too."

"Right."

But she didn't feel reassured when he headed off. She saw his big black truck disappear down the driveway, and her heart felt as if it had tumbled into the pit of her stomach. Something was wrong. Something was bugging Zane, and the sooner they got to the bottom of it, the better off they'd be.

Eve picked up groceries that evening on her way back from the production meeting in Reno. While she diced fresh tomatoes for dinner, Zane sat on the edge of the kitchen table, watching her.

She loved having him in the kitchen with her. He made her feel feminine, even a little domestic, which was quite a contrast to her work as a director.

Warm from standing over the stove, she turned and smiled at him. "I've cooked more in the past two weeks than I have in the past two years."

He leaned back against the table. "Is that a good thing or a bad thing?"

"Good." Eve gave the sautéed onions a quick stir. "It's great to have some balance. I needed it."

"You ever think about the future? What you want down the road?"

"All the time."

"And what do you want?"

"Work. Family. Kids." She smiled again. "The whole ball of wax."

"What if you can't have everything, what would you pick?"

She set the spoon down. "Why can't I have everything?"

His massive shoulders shifted. "Life doesn't work like that."

"Says who?"

"Says life. Look at your dad. Look at Ty. Look at my past."

She didn't like the tone or the direction their conversation was taking. "You're awfully pessimistic tonight."

"Not pessimistic, just realistic. You know you can't have everything. There are always choices to be made. Decisions. Don't tell me you haven't had to make hard decisions to get where you are. I know you've sacrificed a lot—"

"Where's this going?" she interrupted quietly, hating the cold knot forming inside her.

He stood up, restless, and raked a hand through his hair. "I don't know. Maybe that's the problem. I don't know where this is going and it worries me."

"There's no reason to worry. Things are going well. We're doing good. We're happy, aren't we?"

He smiled, yet the expression in his eyes looked bleak. "Happier than I've been in years."

Her heart turned over at the pain in his voice. "Happiness is a good thing, isn't it?"

When Zane saw the concern in Eve's lovely blue eyes, it staggered him, as it always did, that she should care so much for him. He'd forgotten what it felt like to be loved by a woman. Cherished. How being with the right person could make everything so much better. And that's what scared him.

Eve loved him, but she wasn't going to stay. She'd be off soon, traveling, working, keeping crazy hours God knows where. Already he worried about her driving alone at night in big cities. He worried about her going to a dark apartment. Worried about deserted parking lots and late-night errands and all the dangerous situations she'd face on a daily basis.

What if something happened to her? What if someone hurt her? He'd be miles away. He wouldn't be able to do a thing, and he'd already lost one love. He couldn't lose another.

"I'll miss you."

Her eyes met his. "I'll be back, Zane, I promise."

But she didn't understand. She didn't know that it would take just one stupid decision, one bad call, one reckless moment and it would all be over.

I love you, he thought. *I love you so much.* But he couldn't say it. Couldn't say any of the things he was feeling because he knew this: he couldn't come between Eve and her career.

He loved her so much he had to let her go. But until then, he'd be with her, love her, treasure what little time remained.

Zane went to her, drew her into his arms. He slid his hands beneath her knit top and under the edge of her bra. Eve shivered with pleasure and his body responded instantly, hardening. He covered her lips with his, intending to give her a tender kiss, a sweet kiss, but it grew hot and intense immediately.

Unzipping Eve's slacks, he dragged them over her hips and slid her panties down, too. Their lovemaking was wild, frantic, and by the time they'd found release, the pasta sauce had boiled over, splattering chunks of tomato across the entire stove.

CHAPTER FOURTEEN

SHE REALLY LOVED THIS FILM, Eve thought, sitting back one day in the screening room at the hotel. It was working. It was all coming together. Ty had done his best to put his troubled past behind him. He'd grown comfortable with the horses and even insisted on doing a number of his own stunts, including one daredevil riding scene.

But she wasn't the only one pleased. Eve had just finished reviewing the dailies with her director of photography and the sound and lighting directors. They all agreed that they had some good stuff in the can. There should be no problems in the editing room when they got back to Los Angeles.

Eve had always worked hard, always taken pride in her work, but what she felt now was altogether new. She'd really accomplished something here. She'd saved the film, taken a torpedoed ship and pulled it to safe harbor.

Her dad should be here. He should see this.

The lights in the room turned on and everyone began pushing chairs back, heading out, but Eve didn't move.

She'd call home tonight, see if her dad and mom couldn't make it up for a few days. She'd arrange airline tickets for them. Get a room at the hotel. Maybe

Zane would even let them stay at the house. Either way, it'd be great to get her dad on the set.

Zane surprised her when she reached the house by his less-than-enthusiastic response to her plan. He didn't say it was a bad idea, but he definitely didn't offer the use of his house.

"You'll have to meet them, of course," she said, trying to hide the hurt she felt at his indifference.

"If I'm around," he said, going through the paperwork stacked on his desk. "I've got some meetings lined up out of town. Prospective buyers and breeders."

"When will you head out?" she asked, leaning against the door to his den. It wasn't a big room, and had been furnished simply, but the big walnut desk and the green leather chair made it look cozy.

"Well, what if I wait to call them until you know your schedule?"

"Don't do that." He pushed the paperwork away. "Make your plans, get things set, and if I can't meet them this time, maybe the next."

His words were right, but the tone was wrong.

Eve felt her temper rise. He didn't really want to meet her parents. He didn't care about meeting them. In fact, she had a sneaking suspicion that no matter when her parents came, he'd be gone. "You don't intend to meet them, do you?"

She'd folded her arms across her chest, and when he glanced up at her, she knew she looked angry.

His face was expressionless. "If I have plans—"

"Don't lie to me."

They were fighting words. He knew it, too. "Eve, we agreed from the beginning that there were no commitments. I like being with you. You like being with me. Let's just leave it at that.''

"So there isn't a future.''

"I didn't say that.''

"But you don't want to meet my parents.'' *After everything I told you,* she silently added.

She walked out, headed for the bedroom, but stopped midstride when she passed the empty bedroom with the art tables and boxes of mugs.

For a long moment she stood in the hallway and stared at the door.

What was going on here? What was happening with her and Zane? Why didn't he want to meet her parents, and why was he still holding on to Jenny's things? Five years was a long time to leave a room unchanged.

She turned around and headed back to Zane's study. His door was still open, and his head was bent as he read through a stapled document.

"Except for Zach, I've never met any of your family,'' Eve said tightly, "yet everyone lives here in Reno. Your parents. Your sisters. You still see them. You have lunches and dinners and yet you've never introduced me. Why?''

His brow furrowed. "Just hasn't happened yet, that's all.''

And it wasn't ever going to happen, she thought with sudden insight. He liked her, was attracted to her, maybe even loved her, but it wasn't the way she wanted him to love her. He'd put limits on their relationship. She just hadn't realized it before.

Drawing a slow breath, she tried trying to calm herself, to stay focused on the issue foremost in her mind. "When you asked me last week what I wanted from my future, you never told me what you wanted. What is it that you want, Zane? What's important to you?''

He picked up a pen. ''Family.''

Family? But he hadn't introduced her to his, and he didn't want to meet hers.

''I want kids,'' he continued. ''Have a chance to live a normal life like anybody else.''

Eve's heart squeezed so tight she had to bite her lip to keep from crying aloud. ''Do you think I don't want kids?''

''I've never said that. I just know you've made a lot of sacrifices to get where you are. I've watched you at work this month. You put in incredibly long hours.''

There was more he wasn't saying. ''You see my work and motherhood as a conflict of interest?''

''I didn't say that, but you are thirty-five. Women are only fertile for so many years.''

She laughed, but the sound was brittle. ''Clock's ticking, right?''

''It's reality.''

Reality again. Oh, he loved to pull that reality thing on her, didn't he? But what about his reality? What about the guest room with the art table and the paint brushes and the closet full of boxes? How did all those things fit into reality? ''You have double standards.''

''How's that?''

''You tell me to face reality, but what about you? Jenny's gone, but you're still hanging on to the past—''

''I'm not. Her clothes are gone. Her dresser is empty. The only thing I continue to do in her name is support her favorite charity.''

''Then what are those boxes of mugs in her studio?

Why are they still stacked in the closet? What are you going to do with them?''

"What's there to do?''

"Sell them. Put them in a gallery. Let some of Jenny's dreams come true.''

His features hardened. "You don't know the first thing about her.''

"No, but I saw her work. I saw what she made. She didn't paint a hundred mugs so they could sit in a bedroom closet!''

"I don't want to talk about this anymore.''

"You might not want to, but maybe you need to.''

"No, and this is really none of your business.''

Eve tried to ignore the sick feeling in the pit of her stomach. "So why am I here, Zane? Never mind Jenny, what are *we* doing?''

He stiffened yet again. "Good question.''

It dawned on Eve then that Zane wasn't over Jenny, that he couldn't, wouldn't, move on. "You still love her.''

"I'll always love her, but I do know she's gone.''

"Then you also must know that Jenny was an artist. She had a lot of talent. If you loved her half as much as you say you do, you'd find a better home for her work than leaving it wrapped up in a dark closet.''

DURING THE LUNCH BREAK, Ty took a seat across from Eve at one of the tables set up by Catering. The dining tent was crowded and noisy.

"So how are you?'' he asked, sitting down and pushing up the sleeves on his shirt. "How's the boss? You two getting along all right?''

Eve leaned forward, the din of voices and clang of

cutlery making it difficult to hear him. "What makes you ask?"

He tore a chunk off his crusty sourdough bread and dipped it in his bowl of soup. "He's a menace today." Ty popped the bread in his mouth, chewed and swallowed. "Overheard him giving someone an earful earlier."

"Where?"

"In the barn."

Eve lost what was left of her appetite. She pushed her plate away even though she'd barely nibbled on her pasta salad. She'd been wondering about Zane's mood. They hadn't spoken since last night, and they certainly hadn't made love.

"Do you know what's with him?" Ty persisted.

She hesitated. "I brought up his late wife."

"Oh."

"In hindsight it wasn't the smartest thing to do."

"He loves you."

She reached for her iced tea. "But he's not over her."

Ty tore off another chunk of bread and chewed in silence. "I think he is over her," he said after a minute. "I think something else is bugging him."

"I don't know. If you'd seen his face when I mentioned Jen—"

"That face thing, that's just a guy thing. Guys hate *feelings*."

Eve wished she could smile, but she couldn't. "I wanted to bring my dad and mom out to meet Zane, but he's not interested."

"He's afraid. That's got to be it."

"Afraid of what?"

Ty shrugged. "Have you guys talked about the future? Or are you just avoiding it, living in denial and trying to pretend that nothing's going to change?"

"There isn't a future. Zane's made that clear."

"Bullshit," Ty said, pushing away from the table and standing. "Don't believe that for a minute."

There was no time to talk to Zane until Eve called it quits later in the afternoon. They wrapped up earlier than they had in a week, and everybody was looking forward to some free time.

Most of the crew elected to head to McCornick and Weston's in Reno for a drink. Ty still wasn't allowed back in the country-western bar, but Hugh Armstrong and Kate Cooper were heading to dinner elsewhere and included him in their plans.

With everyone cleared out, Eve went in search of Zane but couldn't find him anywhere. It wasn't until she noticed that his truck was gone that she realized he'd left the ranch.

ZANE DIDN'T KNOW WHAT the hell was wrong with him, only that he couldn't go back to the ranch. After finishing up his shopping and banking, he called Zach and talked his brother into meeting him at McCornick and Weston's for dinner and a game of pool.

But dinner and the game didn't help. If anything, Zane felt worse.

"Cut it out," Zach said, slapping Zane on the chest. "Stop moping. You're really irritating when you mope."

"I'm not moping."

"Then what's with the face? Things are great. You and Eve are doing great. I'm so glad you've hit it off."

Zane felt as if he'd swallowed a can of nails. "It's not working out."

Zach almost dropped his beer. "What?"

Zane concentrated on chalking his cue. "It's just not."

"Why not?"

Zane didn't want to do this. He was so tired of justifying himself. "Because we're different people. We want different things. No use dragging this out—"

"She know this?"

Man. The sick feeling just kept getting worse. "I think so."

"You're so full of it."

"Shut up."

"No. Eve's crazy about you. She loves you. She'd probably marry you, have your kids—"

"Can't happen long-distance. She lives in L.A. I live here. I'm certainly not moving."

Zach leaned against the pool table. He stared hard at his brother for a long, silent moment, then his expression cleared, comprehension dawning. "You're scared."

Zane rolled his eyes. "Oh, for Pete's sake. Get real."

"It's true. You're scared of being hurt."

"I'm not scared of being hurt. I'm scared of leading Eve on. I don't want her getting carried away, making big plans when this just isn't going to go anywhere."

"Did something happen between you two?"

"No."

"Did you have a fight?"

"*No.*"

Zach shook his head, as if unable to believe Zane was serious. "So when are you going to tell her?"

"I don't know. When the moment's right." Zane

lifted his stick, leaned over and aimed at the cue ball. "Let's just play. That's what we came here for."

Back at the ranch, Eve's frustration was turning to concern. Zane hadn't come home for dinner. He wasn't even back by the time she changed for bed.

Sitting in the middle of Zane's bed, Eve did her best to ignore the slightly queasy sensation in her stomach, the sixth sense that told her she and Zane had turned a corner in their relationship and it was taking them in the wrong direction.

It was late when at last she heard him come in. He undressed quietly in the dark, disappeared into the bathroom, then, clicking off the bathroom light, returned to the bedroom and climbed into bed.

Eve kept her eyes closed while Zane slid into bed, even as she secretly wished he'd reach for her, wake her up with a kiss.

She'd reach out to him, but she was so afraid of being rebuffed. He'd been so cold about her parents and her desire to have a baby. He'd made her feel small. Inconsequential. She couldn't bear to have him reject her again.

But lying there, she hoped against hope he'd want to hold her, to connect with her. But he didn't. She heard him turn over and pull the covers up, and eventually he fell asleep.

By the time Eve awoke the next morning, Zane was already up and dressed.

No kiss good-night. No morning lovemaking. No intimacy of any kind. Just cold, empty space.

For a long time she lay still, her arms behind her head, and stared at the ceiling.

How funny, she thought, but she knew exactly what was coming next. She could predict not only the ending, but the way it would unfold. She'd been through failed relationships before.

Yet now that she was faced with the end of her relationship with Zane, she couldn't imagine saying goodbye.

Or leaving.

Or ever forgetting.

She'd never cared about love, or living without someone's love, until now.

After she'd dressed, Eve headed to the kitchen, but Zane wasn't there. He had, however, left her a nearly full pot of coffee, and Eve poured herself a cup and made toast.

She ate numbly, drank slowly, keeping her mind intentionally blank. She couldn't let herself lose control. She had to stay focused. Had to get the job done.

Twelve hours later, Eve was finally free to collapse, but she didn't. She waited until everyone dispersed before heading for the house and taking a seat on the front steps. It was time to talk to Zane.

Honey Bear stretched out next to Eve on the top step, content to soak up the last rays of sunshine and periodically thump her tail. Eve rubbed Honey's silky ears. "Do you know what's going on?" she asked the lab. "You know him. What's happening inside his head?"

But Honey just wagged her tail and gave Eve's hand a lick.

They were still sitting there when Zane pulled up in his truck twenty minutes later. Eve watched him walk toward her. "Hi," she said.

"Have a good day?"

"Yes. And you?" My goodness, they were formal.

He stopped and leaned over to scratch Honey behind the ears. "Fine."

"Good." Eve noticed there was no scratch or kiss for her. "Do you have a minute?"

"Depends," he answered, lips curving, but it wasn't a smile. It was anything but a smile.

"I know you're mad at me—"

"I'm not mad."

She tried again. "I upset you, then, bringing up Jenny's mugs. I'm sorry. It was none of my business."

"That's fine. It's over." He stepped over Honey and around her, his boots thudding on the boards. "Is there anything you feel like for dinner?"

Was that it? Were they done talking? *"Zane."*

He turned around, stared down at her. "Do you really want to do this now?" he asked, his voice deepening. "Or can we just not talk about us, or the future, and enjoy dinner together?"

If ever there was handwriting on the wall, she thought, this was it. "Is it that bad?"

His broad shoulders shifted. "We're not going to agree, and time's short. Let's just have the night, enjoy the next week or so, and not figure out what happens when the movie wraps."

But he knew what would happen when the movie wrapped. He'd already decided what would happen. Eve bit down hard on the inside of her cheek. She counted to five, and then ten. "You're essentially saying there's no future."

"I'm saying I don't want to have to decide anything tonight."

"That's not what you're saying...." Her voice faded as she heard him mutter beneath his breath.

"I knew we'd end up fighting."

"We're not fighting—"

"We will."

"Why?" He didn't answer and her eyes burned. She had to force herself not to cry. "You're going to break my heart, aren't you."

"Eve, this isn't love—"

"The hell it isn't." She got to her feet, closing the distance between them. "I do love you. I love you more than I've ever loved anyone."

He turned his head, giving her a stony profile.

Her heart twisted in shapes she didn't think it could. "You don't love me," she whispered, feeling the most awful wrench of emotions. It was almost as if her heart was that door on the cabin and it had just come off in Zane's hands.

"We have a week," he said wearily. "Is this really necessary?"

How could he even ask?

Eve walked away from him, back to the edge of the veranda and the view of the ranch buildings and pastures. Beyond Zane's property lay Zach's, and their combined spread was sizable. Lots of land, lots of sky, lots of room to dream. "So we don't talk now. We just pretend everything's okay, and then when my work here is finished, we'll have the big breakup?"

"That would at least give us more time now."

"More time for what?" She turned to look at him over her shoulder. "To anticipate the goodbye? To check my watch a dozen times a day to see how much time we—I—have left?"

"Something's better than nothing."

Her vestige of calm snapped and hot tears filled her eyes. "But why does it have to be just 'something'? Why can't we have more? Don't we deserve more?"

He shook his head and pushed open the door, holding it for her. "What would you like for dinner?"

They ate in the most miserable silence possible, and by the time the plates were scraped and stacked, Eve knew what she had to do.

While Zane started washing the dishes, she headed to the bedroom, pulled her suitcase from a closet and began to pack. She worked quickly, efficiently, lifting tidy piles of shirts and slacks into her open suitcase. Because she wasn't thinking, and wasn't feeling, she was able to pack nearly everything in just minutes.

As she zipped her soft-sided suitcase shut, she heard Zane's voice behind her. "I told you I wasn't good for you."

Eve was hit by a wave of emotion so strong she had to close her eyes to get her bearings. But even with her eyes closed, the emotions just kept coming—rage, pain, resentment.

"That's not what you really mean," she said, placing the suitcase on the ground by her feet. "When you say you're not good for me, you're not talking about you, you're talking about me. You're really saying I'm not good for *you*."

"I hate it when you put words in my mouth."

She faced him. His gaze had narrowed and his jaw was firm, but she saw confusion in his eyes. He didn't like what was happening, but he wasn't going to stop it. "Well, I hate it when you're not honest, and you're not being honest. You're the one who has a problem with me. You're the one who can't imagine a future with me."

"We're just in different places, Eve. We want different things."

"Is that so?" She wanted to understand. She wanted

to handle this maturely, without hysterics or tears. "What do you want that I don't want?" At least her voice came out even. Good. She'd done something right tonight.

But Zane didn't answer.

Her chest felt as if it was on fire. "I've been so happy just being with you—"

"Eve."

"It's true. I love you. I love being with you. I've loved the way you look at me. I've loved the way you talk to me. I've loved the way you listen to me." She blinked, unwilling to let the tears fall. "Why does it have to change?"

"We have different goals, Eve, different dreams. Your career is your baby, and I...I want a real baby—"

"This is about my career?" Eve heard her voice rise, heard the surge of emotion. Her eyes stung but she blinked the tears back. There was no way in hell she'd cry now.

He didn't look at her, but fixed his gaze on some distant point that had nothing to do with her. "You're a good director."

"Yes."

"You've already signed on for three more films."

It was her career. He had a problem with her work. "Yes."

"You're in demand."

"I've worked so hard to get here. I've worked twelve-, thirteen-hour days for years."

His voice sounded rough. "I know you have."

She bent her head and studied the faded Native American rug on the floor, telling herself that under no circumstance would she cry. Tears were for helpless people. She was not a helpless woman. She was smart and capable and she wasn't going to disintegrate over him.

"It's in your blood," he continued, his voice gathering strength, as well as conviction. "Your dad's a director. Your mom's a makeup artist. You grew up surrounded by show biz people."

Eve picked up her suitcase and walked past him, feeling the bump of her suitcase as it grazed his leg. But she didn't stop, and she didn't apologize. She'd heard enough. She was tired, and if she didn't get the hell out of his place, she'd be bawling like a baby any minute.

It was so not fair, she thought as she reached for the doorknob. He'd decided they couldn't be together because of her career. *Her career.* Not his work, not his isolated ranch, not even the scars he carried from his past life—but *her* career.

How could he?

How could he do this to her when she'd offered him her future? Promised her heart? Did her love mean so little? Did he find her easy to toss aside?

Eve gripped the doorknob so hard her knuckles ached. She had to go. That's all there was to it. She had to get back to work, get on with things, and try to put this last month into perspective.

But turning, she saw him standing behind her in the hallway, his green eyes haunted, his shoulders rigid.

It was crazy, but she knew deep in her heart he loved her, and yet love wasn't enough, at least not in this case.

Eve slowly set her suitcase down. "I do have breaks between films. I can get away on weekends, and you can visit me on the set."

"Sneaking away for a few days here and there isn't much of a relationship."

Why was she doing this? Why was she torturing herself? He'd already made up his mind. It was over. He wasn't going to give her a chance. He wasn't going to try to work something out.

Yet still, she couldn't accept that he'd break her heart like this. "It's not perfect, but it's better than nothing."

"It's not better for me."

Briefly she closed her eyes, thinking of all the times she'd been on location and felt tired, and more than a little bit lonely, at the end of a long day. Many of the crew would have paired up, but Eve would be in her room working, trying hard to stay focused on the film. There were times the hotel rooms and traveling and the constant demands wore her down and she wished she had one person who loved her. One person who missed her. One person who understood the demands of her career and the importance of her dream.

One person who would encourage her no matter what.

One person who'd say, I believe in you. You will not fail.

One person who'd love her if she should fail.

Eve blinked, her eyes swimming. She'd thought he was it. She'd thought Zane was that person.

If only he hadn't been such an amazing lover.

If only he'd said just once that he loved her.

CHAPTER FIFTEEN

DESPITE HER INNER TURMOIL, the next ten days passed
quickly for Eve as they neared the end of their shoot.

She had her own hotel room again and worked late
at night, then woke early to get back on the set. It was
rather ironic that while her personal life felt like a
wreck, the film was coming together beautifully. More
than one person had commented that Ty was delivering an Oscar-worthy performance and she agreed.
He'd absolutely nailed the part of Jack Henry.

Having a big studio behind her did matter, Eve realized. A big studio meant big dollars, and big dollars
could buy the best talent. *American Jack* had been shot
with one of the best cinematographers in the business
and that had made a huge difference in the quality of
the film.

On the last full day of filming, Tim and the co-
producers arrived from Los Angeles. A month ago Eve
would have worried about so many people on the set,
but now it hardly mattered if there were ten people
lurking on the peripheral or a hundred.

Zane's property, however, had taken a beating from
all the trucks, trailers, equipment and parade of cars.
Eve had a contractor and landscape crew standing by
to come in and clean up and make all necessary re-
pairs.

"I've seen the rough outakes," Tim said, standing

by Eve as the crew adjusted the lights and cameras for the last scene of the day. "They're good. Really, really good."

She nodded. "I am pleased."

"This film is going to get some attention." The producer looked at her. "You'll get some serious nods, too. Maybe best director."

"I can't think that far ahead. I'm more interested in getting this edited and scored right." Eve saw the crew was ready for her and she shook Tim's hand. "Thanks for coming. I'll catch up with you and the others at lunch."

That night, with most of the filming wrapped, the cast felt like cutting loose and celebrating. One of the girls from wardrobe pulled out a newspaper and mentioned the county fair. "It's just outside town," she said. "What do you think?"

Nearly everyone decided to go, and Ty hunted Eve down as she was gathering her things to return to the hotel. "You're coming, aren't you, Eve?" he asked. "It's the whole gang. Cast and crew."

She really didn't have it in her to go to a fair. So far she'd been able to hold it together for work, but the moment she let her guard down, the hurt came, and so did the loneliness. She missed Zane, really missed him, and it wasn't even the sex, but the friendship, the energy, the connection. Everything had felt possible with him. "Not tonight, Ty. I've got a lot to do—"

"So does everyone, but it's important to let your hair down and celebrate with your cast and crew. Everyone wants you there," he added quietly. "Everyone's enjoyed working with you."

Eve drove with Ty and her assistant director to the

fairgrounds on the edge of town. It was twilight by the time they arrived, and the sun was just starting to set in the corner of the sky.

Ty paid for everyone's admission to the fair, and purchased long strips of tickets for the carnival rides, doling them out with injunctions to go have fun and remember to meet at the food tent for dinner at seven.

As Ty finished passing out tickets, Eve experienced an odd ripple of awareness, a tingle down her spine that made her feel more than a little vulnerable. Turning, she spotted Zach, Leslie and Zane heading her way.

"You invited Zane?" she said to Ty under her breath.

Ty looked at her with innocent eyes. "Shouldn't I have?"

Her chest felt tight. She hadn't seen Zane in days. He'd avoided her, and the crew, by taking off to California for a few days, but he was back now, and he looked more gorgeous than ever in a black thermal shirt, faded jeans and boots.

Ty greeted Zach and Zane, and was introduced to Leslie.

Zach hugged Eve. "Good to see you again," he said.

"Yes," she agreed, shooting a quick glance at Zane. She felt incredibly self-conscious. She hadn't been prepared to see him like this.

"You two know each other, I believe," Zach added, nudging Zane with his shoulder. "In case you've forgotten, Zane, this is Eve Caffrey, famous film director. Eve, Zane Dumas, Reno's top horse breeder. You guys would probably like each other if you took the time to talk."

Zane finally looked at her—really looked at her—
and the intensity in his eyes unnerved her.

He knew how she felt. He knew what she wanted,
and while he didn't hate her, he wasn't going to love
her, either.

Hugh and Kate pushed through the turnstile just as
they were about to head for the rides. "Sorry we're
late," Kate called out breathlessly. "I was developing
some prints from the photo shoot with Ty and completely lost track of time."

Kate reached into her oversize leather bag and
pulled out a handful of photos. "Check this out," she
said, handing the stack to Ty. "They came out great.
These are just some quickies—they'll look better for
the magazine—but I wanted you to see."

Everyone gathered around Ty to get a look at the
shots for the fashion layout. The black-and-white
proofs were really strong, and very sexy. In several
Ty was dressed in a formal tuxedo, leaning against the
rough split-rail corral. In another, his jacket was off
and tux shirt unbuttoned halfway down, and he was
lying on top of the bunkhouse, smoking, looking up
at the sky.

"Wow." Eve lifted a photo of Ty bareback on a
horse, wearing nothing but slacks. His hair was tousled, he had a hint of a beard, and there were weary
creases at his eyes. The overall effect was stunning.
Very male, very western, very evocative. "They're
terrific. Kate, Ty, these really are lovely."

"Wait until you see my favorite," Kate said.

Ty flipped through another couple of pictures of him
roping and then stopped. This photo wasn't of Ty or
any of the models Kate had hired for visual interest.
This photo was of Eve. She was standing off to one

side, in front of the stable, and wearing a snug white turtleneck that emphasized the smooth lines of her face and the silky blond weight of her hair. There was no one else in the photo, no props, no movement. It was a three-quarter profile shot, and her expression was fixed, serious. She looked tough, strong, self-sufficient—and yet very alone.

"My favorite," Kate said. "You look incredible, Eve. You could be a model."

Eve flushed. Kate was a great photographer and she'd captured Eve in a pensive mood, but Eve didn't want to be reminded that her toughness and independence were what had driven Zane away. "Anyone up for the rides?" she asked, changing the subject. "I haven't been on a roller coaster in years."

With Ty in the lead, they hurled themselves from one carnival ride to another, all seeming to involve spine-jolting twists and turns. After the third herky-jerky roller coaster, Eve was beginning to think she'd had enough.

"Bumper cars?" Ty suggested as the group stumbled breathlessly from the last ride.

"How about baby animals?" Leslie answered, rubbing the back of her neck. "We don't want whiplash."

"I like animals," Ty retorted, "but I've just spent a month on Zane's ranch. I need some thrills."

So they charged ahead and lined up for the bumper cars. At the last moment Eve balked.

"Count me out on this one," she said, taking a position at the guardrail. "I'll watch from here."

"Me, too," Zane said, stepping over the rope and out of the way.

Ty forged on, climbing into a cobalt-blue miniature

car, and Eve noticed that a small crowd had begun to gather at the edge of the ride. Ty had been recognized.

Zane spotted the throng, too, and glanced at the group of curious fairgoers and then back at Ty, who was laughing as he drove his blue car into Hugh's. "He settled down, didn't he?" Zane said, leaning on the rail, his blue denim shirt rolled up to reveal wide tanned forearms.

"He really pulled through. His work is beautiful."

"You're beautiful."

She closed her eyes, held her breath, and tried to quiet the buzzing in her head. How could he do this now? "Let's just stick to safe topics, shall we?"

Zane shot her an apprising glance. "What's safe?"

"The weather?"

"Is that really what you want to discuss?"

She swallowed hard. "No, but it's better than what we discussed last time. If I recall, you didn't like much about me, or my life."

"That's not true, Eve. I admire you. I really respect you."

"As long as I quit my job!"

Her pulse raced and she felt her temper start to rise, but she didn't want to get sucked back into the emotional turmoil again. "There's no reason I can't have a career and be a mother and wife, too. Women do it all the time. My dad was a director and a great parent, and if he can do it, I can do it." She looked at him and his strong profile. "And if you loved me, you'd believe in me, too."

"I do love you."

The right words, the wrong time. Eve turned around and faced the lighted Ferris wheel. The huge ride was lit with neon pink-and-yellow lights and looked like a gigantic wedding cake turned on its side. "You love me?"

"Very much."

She steeled herself against the tenderness in his voice. What good was it if he was going to place conditions on his love? He couldn't control her. He couldn't define her as a woman, either. Eve knew what she could or couldn't do, and he had to trust her on that, too.

He drew a rough breath. "I want to be with you."

"What does that mean? You miss sleeping with me?"

"*No*. We've never been about sex and you know that."

She was tired. Too tired for games, pretense, any of it. From the beginning he'd fought his feelings for her. His reluctance and resistance had finally worn her down. She didn't have the energy to sustain the relationship anymore, not if they weren't equal partners, with a strong commitment to each other.

"Let's not try to make any decisions tonight, Zane. I leave tomorrow. You've known for a while that I'm going, and yet you've waited until the last minute to talk about us—"

"Better late than never," he interrupted tersely.

Was that true? Was there ever a point of no return in a relationship? "I just don't see the point in making any plans or decisions right now. We're both feeling a lot of pressure." But it was more than that, and she knew it. She was angry. Hurt. He'd pushed her away. He'd pushed her *and* her career away.

His expression turned grim. "I didn't think you were a quitter."

"I'm not. But I've been hurt, Zane, and I need some

time, to think. I need some time, period." And that
was the truth. She had to be cautious now, had to
proceed slowly. Eve couldn't bear to get excited or
feel hope again, only to have him push her away once
more in a couple of weeks time.

He was saying all the right things now, but had he
really changed? Or was he panicking at the thought of
her leaving? If it was difficult here on the ranch, the
problems would only intensify once she returned to
Los Angeles. Long-distance relationships weren't
easy, and even if she and Zane did live together, it
wouldn't change the weeks—months—she spent on
location. And Eve wasn't about to give up her work.
Not even for Zane.

The others returned as the bumper car ride finished,
and Eve called it a night. She couldn't do this anymore. She couldn't change the past, absolve Zane of
his grief or guilt, and quite frankly, she was through
worrying about him. It was time she concentrated on
her own needs, and moved on with her life.

Catering spent the next day setting up for the end-
of-production party at Twin Bar Ranch. By the end of
the afternoon, the lawn was filled with picnic tables
covered in crisp red-and-white-check cloths, votive
candles and buckets of red Gerber daises and sunny
black-eyed Susans.

Catering had also set up a bar, dance floor and por-
table barbecue. For three hours the cast and crew ate
and talked, danced and laughed. Now that the film had
been put in the can, everyone felt free, easy. Everyone,
Eve thought, but her and Zane.

She only saw Zane at the end of the evening, when
he put in a perfunctory appearance before disappearing

into the house. An hour later most of the actors and crew had packed and gone.

It was time for her to go, too.

Eve stood in the driveway and took in the last of the party. The caterers were quickly cleaning up, folding chairs and loading the truck. It was over. The filming, the party, the crazy roller coaster of emotions.

She still hurt, but the pain was duller now. When she wasn't around Zane she could almost pretend she was fine. That she'd be fine without him. That what happened between them was just a moment of reckless emotion. Lust. Sex.

No. Never just sex.

Lust, yes, but love, too.

One of the catering crew was walking from candle to candle, blowing each out, and the flickering lights in the garden disappeared one by one.

Zach appeared at her side. Eve turned and smiled at him. "Good party," she said. "You did a great job helping to pull it together."

He nodded, but his expression was strained. "They're waiting for you in Zane's house. Ty's got some gifts to pass out and asked me to track you down."

Her heart squeezed. Zane's house. Just thinking about him, just saying his name was like walking into a wall of nails. She hurt. All over. Eve bit her lower lip to get control over her emotions.

Zach's mouth curved, but it wasn't a smile. "You and Zane still not talking?"

Oh, there was that pain again. That sharp, fierce pain. "We talked a little last night. We're all right."

Liar. She was such a liar. It wasn't all right, yet Eve didn't have a clue how to change that. All she knew was that she couldn't keep putting herself out there, leaving herself vulnerable for heartache.

She wished she and Zane had a different ending, but she couldn't fix this one. There was no director cut. No extra film. No retake. What was *was,* end of story.

"I know he loves you," Zach said.

"Oh, please." Eve managed a brittle laugh. "Don't go there. I can handle the flight back to Los Angeles. I can handle my empty house. I can handle the work. I can't handle talking about Zane."

She left Zach in the drive and walked swiftly toward the house, purpose in her quick stride. She'd go in, be part of the final goodbyes, and then start for home.

Entering the house, Eve discovered the living room still full of people, and she hesitated in the doorway. Hugh and Kate were snuggled together on the couch, Ty sprawled in one of the oversize leather armchairs, and Zach's fiancée, Leslie, curled up in the other. And then there was Zane, standing apart from the others, distant and remote.

"There she is," Ty called out, spotting Eve in the doorway. "Come in, sit down, have a seat," he said, teasingly patting his lap.

Everyone laughed and turned to look at her, but it was Zane's gaze she felt. Zane's attention. She smiled faintly, while on the inside she fought panic. She really didn't want be here right now. It was excruciating being around Zane and acting as if there was nothing between them.

"Come on," Ty entreated again, and Kate jumped up, wrapped an arm around Eve and dragged her into the room.

"Presents," Kate said. "Good ones, too."

She pulled Eve onto the couch next to her and Hugh. Ty scooted a large wrapped gift from behind his chair. "Everybody's gotten their thank-you," he said, "but I have a special one left. I owe a lot—" he broke off, took a breath, his voice husky "—to two true friends. Eve and Zane. The most perfect couple I know."

Eve looked up at Zane and he was staring at her.

Ty stood up, lifted a huge box and carried it over to Zane. "Go ahead," he said. "Open it."

"You want to, Eve?" Zane asked, gesturing at the box. She shook her head and watched as he hesitated, then ripped the paper off.

Opening the lid, he lifted an unwieldy object out. Eve heard Zane's swift intake of breath as he lifted a large bronze sculpture and turned it slowly in his hands.

Three horses running. "It reminded me of my brothers," Ty said, "back when we were still together, and it reminded me of us, that weekend in the mountains. Thank you for standing by me when I needed friends most."

Eve's eyes burned. She watched Zane embrace Ty. It was a big-brother kind of hug, a fierce, warm hug of acceptance and pride.

Ty walked over to Eve. "Thank you," he said, kissing her on the cheek. "You've been brilliant, Eve. You're a real human being."

"Don't make me cry," she warned.

"Promise you'll work with me again."

She felt so tender on the inside. "In a heartbeat." She hugged him. "I'm proud of you, Ty. You did great."

"Don't go away," Zane said. "I've got a little something for everyone. Just a second."

He disappeared from the living room and returned with a stack of gifts. They'd all been wrapped in red-and-white-striped paper and finished with a wide black ribbon.

Zane passed out the boxes, giving one to Eve, Ty, Hugh and Kate while Zach and Leslie looked on.

"You didn't have to get us gifts," Kate protested.

Hugh agreed. "Especially since you're the one we inconvenienced."

"It's not been an inconvenience," Zane said. "I thought it'd be a huge hassle, but in the end, it was fun. I really enjoyed seeing the film come together, and it was remarkable watching Eve at work." He gestured to the gifts. "Everyone who worked on the film here got one of these. The others received theirs earlier. I wanted to wait and give these to you personally. Eve, why don't you open yours first?"

Eve stripped the cheerful paper from the box, and as she pulled away the crisp white tissue, her eyes opened wide. What was he thinking? "This is one of Jenny's mugs."

Zane nodded, and Eve touched the ragged purple mountain painted on the beige background. "You're giving the mugs away?" she asked, perplexed.

"Jen loved the ranch, and I wanted everyone who was here working on the movie to have something special to take home with them. It seemed like a good thing to do. I know Jenny would have approved."

He'd emptied the closet? He'd had all the mugs wrapped for the cast? Her mind couldn't quite take it all in. "It's a lovely gift, Zane. But I'm stunned."

While the others opened their gifts, Leslie stood up,

went to Zane and slipped an arm around his waist. "What he's not telling you," she said, "is that there were still two dozen mugs left over, and a downtown art gallery is going to carry them. The proceeds from the sale of the mugs will go to Jenny's favorite charity, a group that funds horseback riding lessons for children with disabilities. Zane's already cut them a big check."

Zebras don't change stripes, Eve told herself, but Zane had certainly shocked her.

"You were right, Eve," Zane said as Leslie returned to Zach's side. "You've been right about a lot of things. I've been hardheaded, and I'm a slow learner, but I'm trying. You have to know that."

She'd thought she loved Zane when they were together, and making love. She'd thought she loved him when they looked at the stars and imagined the future. She'd thought she loved him when he ended their relationship and she cried herself to sleep. But that love didn't touch what she was feeling now.

The tears she'd fought started to fall, and she wiped them away quickly. She wasn't sad, or regretful, she was happy. Zane was going to have a great life. His ghosts were almost off his back.

She looked at him and discovered he'd been watching her.

"Thank you," she whispered, and he nodded.

"I love it," she added.

Kate was busy comparing her mug to Hugh's. She had a calf on hers and Hugh's had a cowboy roping. "They're too pretty to use," she said, carrying them to the mantel.

"No," Zane said gruffly. "They're meant to be used. Enjoyed. That's why Jenny made them. She wasn't a fussy person. She wouldn't want them collecting dust.''

"She might not have been fussy, but she had a great eye." Kate adjusted the mugs on the mantel, turning them so the bright designs faced out. "There, don't they look—" She broke off and picked up a photograph lying on the mantel. "Whose is this?" she asked, flashing them the old black-and-white picture.

"What is it?" Zane asked, having completely forgotten he'd ever put the photo there in the first place.

"An old snapshot of a young couple." Kate turned the photo over. "It looks as if it was taken in the early sixties."

Zach and Leslie exchanged swift glances and Zach joined Kate at the fireplace. "That's Rose," he said, pointing to the pretty young woman. "Our birth mother. And that, we think, is our biological father."

There was a moment of incredulous silence in the living room before Kate cleared her throat. "You think this man is your *what?*"

"Father. The woman is Rose Rydic, we know that much, and we believe the man with her is our father, although we know nothing about him."

"You two were adopted?" Kate said.

"Sort of," Zach answered.

Leslie slipped her hand into Zach's. "My father delivered Zach and Zane at his clinic in Reno thirty-eight years ago, and Eleanor Dumas took them home."

"So the Dumases did adopt you?" Kate persisted.

"Not exactly," Leslie said, holding Zach's hand tightly. "It was a quiet thing. A…secret."

Kate was looking more and more confused. Eve glanced at Zane, who so far hadn't said a word. "The babies were switched at birth,'' Eve said quietly to fill the uncomfortable silence.

Ty whistled. "Switched?"

Even Hugh was nonplussed. "How's that possible in this day and age?"

Leslie looked positively pained. "It's unethical, and theoretically it shouldn't have happened, but I'm sure my dad believed he was doing the right thing at the time." She drew a deep breath. "Dad had two women in the clinic delivering babies on the same night. Eleanor Dumas's baby was stillborn. Rose Rydic delivered two healthy boys, but she died after giving birth. Dad couldn't bear to tell Eleanor she'd lost another child, and he couldn't see putting these beautiful twin boys into the foster care system."

"So he played stork," Ty summed up.

"Yeah."

Kate was studying the photo again. "Here's the really crazy thing," she said softly, giving the photo a brief shake. "I know this man. He looks like my dad, but it's not my dad." She looked at everyone and then focused hard on Zach and Zane. "I'm almost positive it's my uncle Justin."

There was a chorus of voices, protests and exclamations, but Kate held firm. "It's the same face," she said. "It's the Cooper face, and I've seen photos of my uncle from around this time, I'm sure it's him."

Zach leaned over Kate's shoulder, looked at the young couple, then glanced at Zane. "What do you think?" he asked his brother.

Zane's lips thinned and he shook his head. "Impossible. Too far-fetched."

Kate nodded. "It sounds that way, Zane, but look at his cheekbones and the angle of his jaw." She drew invisible lines with her fingertip across her uncle's face. "Both you and Zach have the same bone structure. Your mouth is a little different, but you're tall like him. Uncle Justin is just a hair under six-three. What are you two?"

"Six foot three," Leslie answered faintly, excitement glowing in her eyes.

Again Zach glanced at Zane, but he wasn't talking. Zach drew a slow breath. "Kate, do you know what your uncle was doing almost thirty-nine years ago? Do you have any idea where he was living? If he was working?"

She nodded and handed the photo to Eve, who obviously wanted a closer look. "Uncle Justin was in school. He was a student enrolled at Boston University."

"It's him," Leslie whispered, touching Zach's arm.

Zach couldn't speak. Zane walked away, moving to the window, and stared out at the dark horizon.

"There's one more thing," Kate added. "The Cooper family is famous for its twins. My dad, John, is Justin's twin brother, and I have a twin sister, Kim. You're Cooper twins. I'm sure of it."

Eve watched Zane at the window, feeling his ambivalence and confusion. She didn't blame him. She was overwhelmed herself. "There's only one thing you can do," Eve said. "You have to meet Kate's uncle Justin and you have to get answers from him."

CHAPTER SIXTEEN

THE LAST THING EVE WANTED to do was go east with Zane, but he cornered her as everyone was leaving. "It was your idea for Zach and me to meet this Justin Cooper. You should go with us."

Crash a family reunion? Definitely not high on her priority list. "This is pretty personal, Zane. You're meeting your biological father."

"I never wanted to meet him. I didn't want any of this. But Zach and I could use your company. You're good with people. You can manage stressful situations—"

"Zane—"

"Leslie can't make it," he continued as if she hadn't spoken. "You already heard her tell Zach there was no way she'd get time off from the hospital, and I can't ask Mom, Dad or Melinda to go. This is hard enough on them as it is. Mom's still reeling from the shock of learning we're not really hers."

Eve could believe that, but it just seemed weird to head with Zane to Cooper's Corner when they were just going to part ways twenty-four hours later. "I haven't even met your family here, Zane. Doesn't it seem a bit peculiar for me to go and meet these others first?"

"You want to meet my family? Fine. I'll call everyone, we'll have dinner tomorrow night, and then you'll understand why going to Cooper's Corner is hard for me. I've got a family here. I love my family here. I wouldn't even consider meeting this Justin Cooper if it weren't for Zach, but since it's important to him, I'll go.''

His troubled green gaze met hers. ''But this is hard for me, and I'd love for you to go. I'd feel better if you were there. Please, Eve, don't say no.''

How could she after that?

Three days later they boarded a plane for Boston and took a taxi from there. Their route took them into the Berkshire Mountains, past rolling farmland and quaint New England towns with white clapboard houses and soaring church steeples. After exiting the main highway, they finally arrived at the tiny village of Cooper's Corner. Following Kate's directions, they turned onto an oak-lined drive, and Eve caught a glimpse of a rambling farmhouse through the trees.

They'd spent less than five minutes in Cooper's Corner, but Eve was already hooked. She could picture a movie shot in the Berkshires.

Maybe it wouldn't have hurt to stay the night, or even through the weekend, but she'd made her plans, and it was too late to start canceling everything now. Once Zach and Zane got through the initial Cooper introductions, she'd be heading off, taking a cab back to Boston to catch her red-eye flight home.

''Twin Oaks,'' Zach said from the front seat, indicating the tree-lined drive. ''Just like Kate was telling us. The family plants a pair for each set of Cooper twins.''

''I'm not sure I like all this twin stuff,'' Zane said darkly. ''One twin is enough. I don't need a whole pack.''

As crazy as Zane made her, she was going to miss him. No one delivered a line the way he did. "Twins are people, too," she said, unable to resist poking fun at him.

"Says who?"

She laughed softly. "Well, your brother's human. Leslie said so, and she's a doctor, so she should know. But come to think of it, the jury's still out on you."

The driver slowed and parked in front of the rambling white farmhouse, which was now a bed-and-breakfast. No sooner had he popped the trunk than the front door of the house flew open and people crowded out.

"There's Kate and Hugh," Zach said, picking out the two from the cluster on the steps. "Kind of surreal to think Kate's our cousin."

"*If* she's our cousin," Zane corrected.

Zach glanced back, and his gaze locked with Zane's. "I was really looking forward to this until now. Leslie and I've spent so much time trying to get answers, discover the truth—"

"It's fine, Zach," Zane soothed. "You're just nervous."

"Yeah, but I still want to throw up."

Zane couldn't hide his smile. "Thank God. You're not perfect after all."

Zach cracked a smile.

"Come on," Zane said, grabbing the door handle. "We can do this. We're here. Let's just get it over."

The old farmhouse had been painstakingly restored to a B and B, and Clint Cooper, who ran Twin Oaks with his sister, Maureen, took Eve on a brief tour while Zach and Zane carried the luggage to the rooms reserved for them.

"A film director?" Clint said as they returned to the large gathering room. "Have you worked on anything I'd recognize?"

"Various films, but you'd probably know the production we're just wrapping. *American Jack*—"

"By L. M. Davis. It's one of my wife Beth's favorite books. You're directing the film?"

Eve nodded, finding it hard to talk about the movie right now, hard to think about anything but her flight in six hours and the fact that she'd soon have to tell Zane she was leaving.

She dreaded the goodbye, knew it would be awkward and emotional for her. Even if she acted like an ice princess on the outside, she'd be shriveling up on the inside. When it came to Zane, she was anything but controlled.

"Isn't that Australian actor, Ty-something, starring in it?"

Eve realized Clint was asking a question about the movie. "He is," she said, forcing her attention back to the conversation. "He's done a great job. See the movie if you can."

Zach, Zane and Maureen were heading back down the stairs, but it was Zane's gaze that met Eve's and just like that, she felt the current again, the crazy sense that she and Zane were connected.

She didn't understand what he did to her, but it was potent. Intoxicating. Even after all that had happened between them, she still felt so much.

For better or worse, Zane owned her heart.

Maureen led Zach and Zane into the spacious gathering room. "Dad should be here any minute," she said. "He stepped out on a quick errand. We didn't think you'd get here on time. All the flights have been running late.''

"No problem.'' Zach shoved his hands into his pockets. "We're just glad to be here. We've got a million questions—''

"So do we!'' Maureen interrupted with a quick laugh. "Imagine discovering we have twin brothers in Reno. I didn't believe Kate, couldn't believe it was true, but looking at you two…'' Her voice faded and she glanced from Zach to Zane and then Clint, who stood as tall as the Dumas twins but didn't carry quite as much muscle.

The family connection was obvious. It wasn't just their size, but their facial features, the cowlick in their hair, even the color of their eyes.

"I just wish Dad would get here—''

"I'm here,'' a deep voice said from the doorstep. Justin Cooper stood there in the late afternoon light, his broad shoulders practically filling the door frame, his hair still thick and liberally streaked with gray.

There was a moment of silence as he took in the three men standing next to one another, shoulder to shoulder. "Incredible,'' Justin murmured. "It's too incredible for words.''

It was Justin's suggestion that he, Zach and Zane talk in private at first, but Zane wasn't sure he wanted to go into the library and close the door. He might be built like these Cooper men, but he didn't know what he was supposed to feel. He'd been raised a Dumas. He'd grown up working beside Hamilton on the Twin Bar Ranch.

"This isn't easy,'' Justin said, once the three of them were sequestered in the library. "I didn't know what to think when Kate phoned me in France, but I couldn't ignore her call.''

"What did Kate tell you?" Zach asked.

"Not a lot. Just that she'd discovered a photo of me at your ranch in Reno. She said I was standing with a young woman on the campus of Boston University. Kate asked if I'd ever dated a Rose before, and I knew I had to get on the plane. Had to see you two for myself.''

"And?" Zane asked, torn between ambivalence and wonder. He'd never wanted this meeting. He hadn't cared about finding lost family, but now that he'd come face-to-face with Justin Cooper, he was overwhelmed.

Justin's brow creased. "I wasn't sure Kate had her facts straight, but seeing you two, there's no doubt in my mind. You're my boys. Rose and my boys." He shook his head. "To think I never even knew you existed. Thirty-eight years old and I'm just meeting you now.''

Zach looked perplexed. "What happened?"

"Between Rose and me?" Justin shrugged. "Life. Goals. Different dreams pulling us in different directions." His jaw tightened. "In hindsight, it shouldn't have. There was no reason we couldn't have worked it out, no reason she couldn't have had her career and I have mine.''

"Not many women had careers then," Zach said.

"But Rose was never like other women." Justin moved to the brick fireplace. "I met her while I was in graduate school. She was incredible. Truly beautiful, and she had a voice like you wouldn't believe—'' He broke off, looked up. "Do either of you sing?"

"Zach does," Zane said.

"Zane, too," Zach answered. "He's just pretending to be modest."

Justin smiled wryly. "You two sound like Coopers already. You won't have any problem getting along with Maureen and Clint." His smile faded. "Four kids. I have *four* kids. I always wanted a big family. Must be the teacher in me. I just wish Rose had told me…. I can't believe she'd keep you from me."

"I don't know that Rose would have kept us secret once we were born," Zach said flatly. "She didn't have a chance to make any big decisions, though. She died giving birth."

"She died?" Justin repeated. "She's been gone all this time?"

"She's buried in Reno."

Justin slowly rubbed his jaw. "I had no idea she was pregnant. I should have gone after her. I should have—" He broke off. "I screwed up."

All the should haves, all the guilt, all the things that could have been but weren't. Justin was saying all the things that Zane felt. It was the strangest thing, but Zane recognized himself in Justin Cooper and felt a kinship with him.

"I never loved anyone like I loved her. That's not to say I didn't love Maureen and Clint's mom, because I did, but Rose…" The elder Cooper shook his head, his voice fading. "Rose was that once-in-a-lifetime love. After she headed west, I considered going after her a number of times, but I didn't. Pride held me back. *Pride.* And to think she was pregnant with twins, and alone. She was so young. She must have been scared."

"But she wouldn't tell you, would she?" Zane guessed, thinking of Eve.

"No. Rose wasn't the type to act helpless. She didn't need to lean on a man. She wanted to make her own decisions—" Justin swallowed hard. "I think in some ways I was too young, too. I wish I knew then what I know now. You know, a strong woman is to be admired. A strong woman is a good thing."

Zane felt a lump grow in his throat. He'd never cared about Rose, never felt her loss, but he could suddenly see her for the first time, see his mother as a young woman in search of her dream. He saw the suitcase. The girlish dresses. Her name in lights.

Eve was older, but she wasn't that different from his mother. She was another beautiful woman in search of a dream.

He thought of the photo Kate had given him, the one she'd taken of Eve alone, standing in front of his stable, her face a study of concentration.

His Eve. God, he loved her. And yes, she was a strong woman, but he couldn't bear for her to be alone. He didn't want her to be like his mother. If she needed to travel for work, then he'd be the place she'd call home. If she had a flight to catch, he'd take her to the airport and be waiting for her return. If she should shoot for the moon and fail, well, he'd pick her up and tell her to try again.

There was no other way it would work. He couldn't protect his heart. He couldn't protect her. The only thing he could do was love her. Support her. Encourage her.

Eve had been right. He couldn't have stopped the big rig from piling into his truck. He couldn't have saved Jenny. But it had been five years. He'd loved and lost, and now he was ready to love again.

Correction, he was ready to *live* again.

"I'm sorry," Justin said, turning around again, his green eyes filmed with tears. "I feel like I robbed you of both your mother and father. At the very least, I should have been there for you. I should have been a father to you like I was for Clint and Maureen."

For the first time since all this crazy switched-baby thing started, Zane felt peace. People could only be what they could be. And wasn't hindsight always twenty-twenty? "It's okay," he said quietly. "Eleanor and Hamilton have been great parents. We haven't lacked for anything."

"I hope I'll get to meet them soon," Justin said quietly.

Zane blinked, surprised by the tears stinging his eyes. He hadn't cried in years, yet the tears welled fast and hot, coming from a place deep inside him.

He didn't need a second chance. He didn't need to start over, he just needed to get a move on. Life was short, time was fleeting, and love was everything.

ZACH, ZANE AND JUSTIN COOPER remained in the library for nearly two hours. It was getting late. Eve glanced at her watch. Her cab would be arriving before too long.

How did the day pass so quickly? There'd been a long visit with Hugh and Kate, and introductions to Maureen's twin girls and Clint's wife, Beth, and his son, Keegan. Eve was sorry not to meet Chance Maguire, the father of Maureen's twins, but he was in Europe on business. The afternoon was nearly gone now. Long rays of yellow light fell through the downstairs windows, streaking the floor.

What was she going to say to Zane? They had come so close to getting it right, but when all was said and done, the two of them were different people, and as Zane said, they had different dreams. As much as Eve loved Zane, she couldn't give up her work. It was too much a part of her.

More specifically, what would Zane do in Hollywood? There weren't any ranches off the Interstates 405 or 10, and he was a man who needed land around him. He craved space and solitude. Zane would hate L.A. He'd hate the noise and crowds and smog and snarled traffic. Eve didn't love those things, either, but they went with the job.

Eve checked her watch yet again—

"Going somewhere?"

She hadn't heard the library door open, or Zane approach. Eve shook down her sleeve, covering her wrist. Her heart thumped uncomfortably. "I've got a plane to catch." She saw Zane's pained expression. "I wasn't going to leave without saying goodbye."

He was so quiet, so focused. He was like that as a lover, too. Aware. Attuned. Making love with him had been the most beautiful thing she'd ever known, and she'd have given anything to be in his arms one more time. But it had never happened. She couldn't let it happen. It would only make leaving harder. As close as they were physically, he didn't have a clue what made her tick emotionally. "You and Zach are going to be all right here. The Coopers are great people. You fit right in."

His gaze narrowed. "You make it sound like a wash. I lose you but I get them."

"That's not what I mean—"

"Don't go. Spend the weekend here with me. Let's talk, really talk."

"What about? You don't like my work. You don't

like that I travel. You don't want a wife who will always be leaving, never mind leaving you and the baby." Cheeks hot, she looked at him. "I'm right, aren't I?"

His eyes were somber. "I would rather have a limited amount of time with you than not have you at all."

"You say that now, but you're thinking short term. I know this business. I know how tough it is, how competitive, how hard on marriages. Unless you're sure, very, very sure, it'd never work."

"Maybe I'm sure."

She laughed. *"Maybe?"*

"Can't you see I'm trying?"

She flushed. "I'm sorry. I don't mean to be cynical, but I've lost the rose-colored glasses. You did such a good job pointing out why we wouldn't work, and you were right. We had a fling. One of those hormone-charged romances that occurs on location. It happens all the time." *But never to me.*

"I wasn't on the set." Zane's brows drew together. "I'm not an actor. I was on my ranch, at my home. When we made love, we were in my bed."

She exhaled slowly and stared out the front at the drive and the border of oak trees. "You'll find someone else, Zane, someone from Reno. Someone who knows how to manage a ranch—"

"I'd rather have my movie girl."

Her throat tightened. "You don't know the first thing about making movies."

"I know you."

A yellow cab pulled up in front of the bed-and-breakfast, and Eve's heart fell. "You don't know me."

"I do. I know more than you think."

"Really?" She looked up at him, tears shimmering in her eyes.

He nodded. "I know you broke your thumb when you were ten, punching the boy next door when he called your dad a name. I know you had this crush on some rock star's kid and you used to ride your bike past his house, hoping he'd notice you. He never did."

She ducked her head and dashed away a tear. "Who told you?"

He reached out and touched her cheek, his fingers gentle. "I know you cried when you changed your name, and you promised that one day you'd be a Kowalski again. I know what you want, and, Eve, I want it for you, too."

"*Stop.*" Tears blurred her vision. "Don't do this to me now. The cab's here. The meter's running."

"So? It's just money."

"Don't make this harder than it is—"

"Don't make it harder? Why not? You think I should just let you walk away without a fight? Is that the way men in Hollywood act?"

"You didn't want me two weeks ago."

"Bullshit. I was confused. I needed time to sort things out. I'm allowed to make a mistake, aren't I?"

She hated the damn lump filling her throat. She hated it when others were more reasonable than she was. Wasn't she supposed to be in charge, the one making the decisions? Hell, she was the director. "I guess you can be human if you want."

"Good, because I want. And I want you. I want to be with you, I want to live with you, I want to make love with you. I want to make babies with you." He drew a deep breath. "Am I getting through?"

"I understand you have a lot of wants," she answered in a small voice.

And damn his gorgeous hide, but he started to laugh. "Eve, you might as well send the taxi away. You're not going anywhere tonight."

"I'm not going to send the driver away. He can sit there. It's just money."

"Nie wyglupiaj sie."

Eve blinked. "What?"

"You heard me."

"That's some of the worst Polish I've ever heard."

"It's not an easy language to speak."

Eve struggled not to smile. "And when did you start learning Polish?"

Zane lifted her small suitcase. "I haven't started yet," he said, heading for the stairs. "I've just picked up a few phrases here and there."

"Picked up Polish phrases? How? Where?" She stood in the hall and watched Zane carry her suitcase up. "And for your information, you're going the wrong direction."

He just kept walking.

Eve scrambled up the stairs. "Give me my suitcase."

"Uparciuch," he said, pausing on the second-floor landing. "I bought a little tape thingy. I've been listening to it as I drive."

"Well, stop. You're mangling a beautiful language, and I'm not a hothead."

Zane sighed and shook his head. "Your dad said you'd be impossible. He said you'd drag your heels, put up a fight, that ever since you were a little girl you've been an *uparciuch,* but he also said you feel things deeply. And once you love, you never stop.

So—'' he looked down at her ''—remind me which room is ours.''

He didn't wait for her to tell him. He just set off with suitcase in hand. Eve chased after him. ''You talked to my dad?''

Zane opened one door, peered inside and shut it. ''Wrong room.''

''Zane, you talked to my dad.''

He opened another door. ''I said that already, didn't I?''

She stepped in front of him. ''When did you talk to him?''

''When we had lunch in L.A.''

''You had lunch with Dad?''

He reached over her head, flicked on the light. ''Ah, our room. I recognize my luggage. It's kind of old. I'm going to need some new pieces if I'm traveling more.''

''Traveling?''

Zane pushed the door the rest of the way open and tossed her suitcase onto the bed. ''Well, there's the move to the new ranch—''

''New ranch?''

He cocked his head. ''Is there an echo in here?''

''Zane!''

''Yes, darlin'?''

''What are you talking about? What ranch? What traveling? When did you have lunch with my dad?''

''The Arabian ranch I'm considering buying outside Santa Barbara. The trips we'll take when you're on location. And last week, when I flew to California to meet your parents.'' He circled her waist with his hands. ''Now, no more questions. We're out of time.''

''We've got a lot of time,'' she whispered as his

head dropped lower. "If I'm not catching that flight, and it looks as if I won't be catching that flight, then we can—"

His lips touched hers, silencing her, and Eve felt as if fireworks were exploding beneath her skin. His kiss was as slow and seductive as they came. He kissed her as if they had all day...all night.... "Why don't we have time?"

He lifted his head to look into her eyes. "Because there's something else I'm dying to do, and it isn't talk. Eve, you use ten times the words I do, and as much as I love you, I'm worn out."

"But about my dad," she protested, and then sighed as he slid a hand beneath her blouse and unclasped her bra. "You liked him?"

"I liked him."

"Really?"

His tongue flicked the inside of her lip. "Really. He even gave me his secret borscht recipe, and by the way, in Polish, it's spelled *b-a-r-s-z-c-z*. Let's just make sure our kids get it right. I don't want any beet soup confusion in my family."

She laughed, then gasped as he caressed her nipple between his thumb and forefinger. She loved the feel of his hand against her breast, and the incredible heat of his skin, which even now felt like pure energy. The man made physics beautiful. "Damn, you're good with your hands."

"I know. It's one of my strengths."

She couldn't help laughing yet again. Somehow he'd done it—he'd managed to find the right tone, the right words, the right everything.

"Leslie and Zach are planning a wedding this spring," he said, his lips trailing fire down her neck.

"We could tag along and do a double wedding kind of thing."

"Oh, *twin* stuff."

He laughed softly against her nape. "You have a problem with twins?"

"Not necessarily."

"Good, because you know, twins do run in my family."

"So I've found out."

"Marry me, Eve."

She wrapped her arms around his neck. "Thought you'd never ask."

He was kissing her again, deeply, passionately, and his hands were busy stripping off her blouse.

There was a knock on the door. "Hey, guys." It was Zach, and he cleared his throat. Loudly. "I wasn't sure what you wanted to do about the taxi. The driver's getting impatient. Said to tell you the meter's still running."

Zane's eyebrow rose. "It's your call, Eve. You're the famous director."

She kissed Zane for one long, blissful moment before lifting her head to shout, "You'd better pay him, Zach. It looks like I'm staying the night."

EPILOGUE

"LIGHTS," EVE CALLED, blowing a wisp of bangs from her eyes. It was hot, unseasonably hot for this time of year, and nothing was going right. "Guys, where are the lights?"

"Blew a fuse," one of the technicians shouted back, his shaggy blond head buried in the truck. "Give us a minute. We'll have 'em working in no time."

They didn't have a minute, though. The limousines would be arriving any moment. There'd be forty-some VIPS here any second and Eve wanted everything perfect.

Okay. She took a deep breath, calmed herself. If she couldn't do anything about the lights, she'd check on catering.

Heading toward the lavish buffet tables, Eve passed the sound crew still struggling with the mammoth outdoor system. It wasn't working yet, either. Not good.

As she reached the elegant buffet table, groaning with cheese trays, fruit trays, iced shrimp, stuffed grape leaves, Eve spotted a grubby hand grabbing a fistful of fruit.

"Danny!" she reproached, lightly tapping the hand packed with grapes. "Not ten. Two."

"They're for Dax," Danny protested, opening his hand to show her the red grapes. "Dax."

Eve bit back a smile. Dax and Danny were always

into something, and usually together. "Where is your brother?" Danny just grinned.

"Danny, Grandpa Cooper and Aunt Maureen and Uncle Clint and everybody are going to be here any minute. Where's your brother?"

There was a peal of laughter beneath the table. She should have known. The twins were never far apart.

Eve lifted the pale pink tablecloth and, crouching down, peeked under. "Hello, Dax."

"Hi, Mommy."

His cheeks, still plump with baby fat, were even fuller with a mouthful of grapes. She found his juicy grin irresistible. "How many grapes is that?"

"Hundred million."

"I think that's about one million too many. No more grapes, or you're going to get a tummy ache. And then you won't be able to play with your cousins." She arched her eyebrows. "Those crazy Dumas girls are coming."

"Molly and Meghan?" Danny brightened, popping one last grape into his mouth.

"Yes. Molly and Meghan, and you know how much they love visiting our ranch." She stood, brushed her long skirt smooth. "And if we do go to the beach later, you're going to want to swim, but you can't swim if your tummy hurts."

Dax and Danny exchanged glances and tore off, cowboy boots clomping, kicking up dust.

"Only two and a half years on the job, Mom, and you're already an old pro."

Eve turned and spied Zane lifting a handful of stuffed olives from the buffet table. He was wearing jeans and a casual button-down shirt, and he looked tan, fit, sexier than sin. "Not you, too."

"What can I say? Runs in the family."

She bit the inside of her cheek to keep from laughing aloud. For heaven's sake, someone had to have some control around her! "Speaking of family, they're going to be here any minute—forty-plus Coopers and Dumases, and two Kowalskis—but we've got no lights and the sound crashed—"

"Relax," Zane interrupted, drawing her into his arms and giving her a slow kiss. "This isn't a big-budget production, honey. It's just family."

She curled her fingers against his chest. Even now, after three and a half years of marriage, she was still wildly in love with him. "I know, but I want everything perfect."

He kissed her again, his hands sliding down to cup her bottom. "Just being together is perfect. I love how much you love my family, and I love how you've helped bring us all together. It's going to be a great reunion."

He paused as a fleet of limousines appeared in the drive, passing the whitewashed fences and tidy pastures of the ranch. "And they're here."

As if on cue, the strands of bright colored lights strung overhead lit up.

"Lights!" Danny crowed, running toward them.

The system engineer flipped a switch and music poured from the speaker.

"Sound!" Dax shouted, chasing after Danny and tackling his twin brother to the ground.

Another close one.

Eve turned in Zane's arms and smiled at her boys. Zane was right. Everything was going to be perfect.

"Action!"

Harlequin Romance®

Delightful
Affectionate
Romantic
Emotional

Tender
Original

Daring
Riveting
Enchanting
Adventurous
Moving

Harlequin Romance®—
capturing the world you dream of...

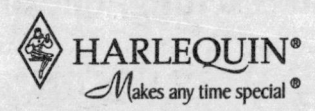

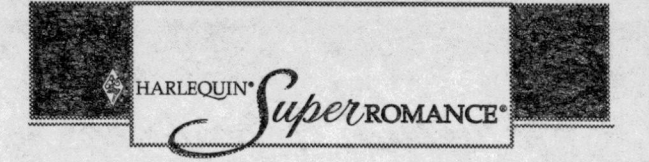
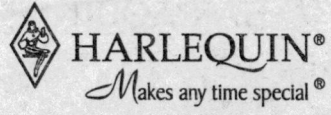

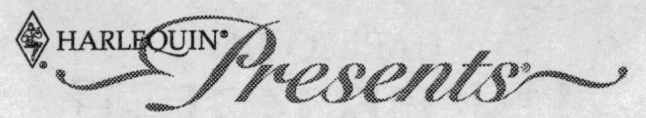

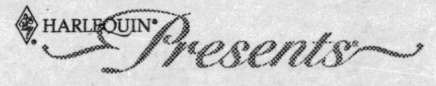

HARLEQUIN®
INTRIGUE

WE'LL LEAVE YOU BREATHLESS!

If you've been looking for thrilling tales of
contemporary passion and sensuous love stories
with taut, edge-of-the-seat suspense—then
you'll love Harlequin Intrigue!

Every month, you'll meet four new heroes
who are guaranteed to make your spine tingle
and your pulse pound. With them you'll enter
into the exciting world of Harlequin Intrigue—
where your life is on the line
and so is your heart!

THAT'S INTRIGUE—
ROMANTIC SUSPENSE
AT ITS BEST!

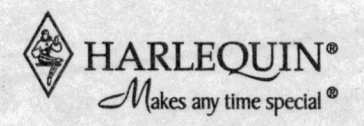

HARLEQUIN®
Makes any time special ®

Harlequin® *Historical*

From rugged lawmen and valiant knights to defiant heiresses and spirited frontierswomen, Harlequin Historicals will capture your imagination with their dramatic scope, passion and adventure.

Harlequin Historicals . . . they're too good to miss!

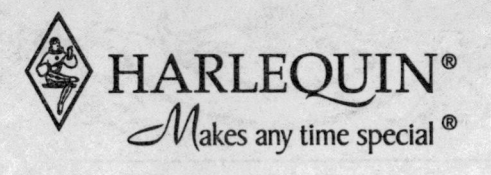

HARLEQUIN®
Makes any time special®

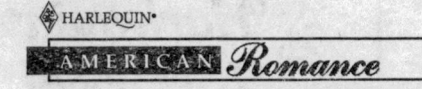

Upbeat, All-American Romances

HARLEQUIN®
Duets™

Romantic Comedy

**Harlequin®
Historical**

Historical, Romantic Adventure

HARLEQUIN®
INTRIGUE

Romantic Suspense

Capturing the World You Dream Of

HARLEQUIN®
Presents

Seduction and passion guaranteed

HARLEQUIN® *Super* ROMANCE®

Emotional, Exciting, Unexpected

Sassy, Sexy, Seductive!

HDIR1